The Golden Shoe

Orphans of the Citadel: Book Two

Michael Owens

Pepperback Press, Inc.

What has come before

Honoring her mother's last wish, Maisy travels to join her marine captain father on the Citadel, an ore processing plant built into the side of an asteroid at the edge of known space. Maisy arrives to find that the coalition government has pulled out of the rim and the marines now report directly to the Citatech Corporation. Changes are swift.

When her father is killed defending a freighter from pirates, Maisy finds herself on a list of "undesirables" and takes refuge with her neighbor's young daughter, Joanie, in the bowels of the station along with many others. There she meets a teenage girl named Lori, who is caring for her infant brother after both of her parents have been arrested.

When the fugitives are swept up and forced onto a shuttle, they are reunited with their parents. Violence breaks out during the transfer and Lori's parents are killed and Maisy receives confirmation from the survivors of her father's crew of his death.

Maisy and her friends are now on the freighter that her father died protecting, under the command of a bitter, angry captain. They are told that they are being taken to an uncharted planet, where they will be dropped on the surface as "colonists." They quickly realize that they are unlikely to reach the planet due to the heavy damage the freighter suffered during the pirate attack. As the engines begin shutting down, the captain decides to abandon the colonists to their fate and flee in the only shuttle.

Realizing his actions would be a death sentence, Maisy and the other passengers thwart the captain's plan and instead place him and the loyal members of his crew in an emergency pod. The remaining crew choose to join the passengers on their journey to 761.

Contents

Prologue

The ship was burning.

Dropping the fire extinguisher to the deck, Marcus ran for the bridge. He made it five meters down the corridor before flames shot out from a panel above him. This time he ducked and kept running.

There were too many fires in too many places to fight them one by one.

Careening onto the bridge he slammed his hand down on the fire suppressant control. As the damage reports began cycling onto the main display, he activated the emergency distress beacon and opened a wide channel.

"This is the *Oro Zapato II*. We are under attack by hostile forces." He released the comm and took a calming breath before starting again. "Repeat, we are under attack. If you are receiving this transmission, we need assistance. We are entering the Simon Belt, two light minutes from the primary base of Citatech Mining Operations."

A soft hand landed on his shoulder. "Marcus, there's nobody out there. At least not close enough to help us. We're on our own."

Marcus laid his hand over his sister's, muting the comm but keeping the channel open. "I can't give up, Cecilia." He glanced up at her face, the soot on her cheeks tracked with tears. Leaning forward, Marcus started again. "Mayday, repeat, we are under attack. This is the *Oro Zapato II* on route from Gamma 367. We are under attack by an unidentified ship."

"We know exactly who they are–" Cecilia was cut off as another alarm ripped through the bridge and the deck beneath their feet lurched.

Marcus clung to the console before him as Cecilia tumbled to the deck. When the ship righted itself, Marcus jumped up to help his sister to her feet.

"Check environmentals," he ordered as he pulled up the engineering damage report.

Marcus stared at the data, his brain refusing to process the information displayed there. Cecilia was talking, but he couldn't hear her over the roaring in his ears. There were two engines offline, but the ship schematic had a blank spot where engine four should be.

It wasn't damaged. It was gone.

Jacob.

Cold sweat beaded on Marcus' brow as he leaned closer to the readout. Jacob had been on the engineering deck. With a shaking hand, he opened a comm channel.

"Jacob?" Silence. "Jacob, it's Dad. Please report your location." The line crackled with static. Cecilia sat frozen beside him, horror growing on her face.

Marcus switched the comm to shipwide. "This is Marcus. Everyone sound off. One."

"Two," Cecilia's voice echoed from behind him and over the comm.

"Three" came the immediate response from his wife, Estelle, in the cafeteria with their grandchildren.

"Four." Marcus's oldest son, Edward, in medical.

Then silence.

Marcus counted. *One...two...three. God, no.*

"Six." Jenny, Cecilia's wife.

"Seven." Harlan, his nephew.

"Eight," sobbed Jacob's wife, Bianca.

The crew of the *Oro* counted down until there was another pause. *One...two...three.* Gia, Harlan's wife, didn't answer. Finally, Estelle accounted for the children.

Jacob and Gia were gone, along with engine four.

Numb, Marcus glanced at the engineering panel again and tabbed up to the outputs. They had lost 17% of their velocity in the last couple of minutes. Laser fire was continuing to eat away at their stern.

"Cecilia, we need to get more power to the other engines or we're not getting out of here," Marcus said hoarsely.

His sister reached out and squeezed his hand, and opened a comm line to her wife. "Jenny, meet me on the engineering deck." She was already up and out of her chair when the response came.

"I'm already here. Bianca is with me." There was a pause. "There's a bunch of slagged metal blocking the corridor and we can't get through. We're going to work our way around it to see the damage on the other side. You stay on the bridge and we'll keep you posted."

"Engine four is completely gone," Cecilia enunciated carefully as she sank back into her chair.

The comm line crackled faintly.

"Understood," Jenny finally said.

"We're coming up to the bridge," Estelle broke into the channel. "Non-essential personnel, meet on the bridge."

"Estelle–" Marcus tried to interject.

She cut him off firmly. "I don't want to hear it. I know as well as you do what our chances are. If we're going down, we're going down together."

"On my way, Mom," responded their son Edward. "I'll bring a med kit."

Marcus ran his hand over his face, elbows on the console, and fought back tears. Estelle was right, they should be together. Taking a deep breath, he opened the wide comm channel again as his family and crewmates began filing onto the bridge.

"This is the *Oro Zapato II*. We are under attack. I say again, this is the *Oro Zapato II* and we are under attack."

Behind Marcus, Estelle herded the children onto the bridge, the youngest on her hip. Harlan ran in a minute later and pulled him into his arms, sobbing into his son's hair as Estelle wrapped her arms around him.

Marcus' voice wavered. "If anyone is receiving this transmission, we need assistance. We are a family ship, with twelve children on board. I repeat, we have twelve children on board. Mayday, mayday..."

As he paused for breath a signal popped up on his panel. Tuning and enhancing the broadcast, he couldn't believe his ears.

"...*Sky*, responding to your hail. Hang on, *Oro*. We are moving to intercept your pursuers."

"Oh my god, thank you!" Marcus held out a hand to Estelle, who threw her arms around his neck with a cry. Turning back to the comm, he continued, "We've lost three of our engines and two members of our crew, including our first mate, my son."

The bodies pressed together at the back of the bridge took a collective breath as Marcus pressed the back of Estelle's hand against his mouth and fought for control of his voice. "We're redlining the remaining engines to maintain our distance but we can't hold it much longer."

"We've got you, *Oro*," came the immediate response. "Hang on for another...twenty-one minutes."

Marcus met his wife's gaze. "I honestly don't know if we can."

"We will do what we have to," Estelle whispered to him firmly, giving him another squeeze before letting go.

"*Oro*, can you change course thirty-seven degrees starboard, eleven degrees down? That will cut down our intercept time to...fourteen minutes."

Marcus nodded to Cecilia, who tapped the coordinates into the console. "We'll lose some of our distance, but yes, we can do it. Executing now."

The deck of the *Oro* vibrated alarmingly as the remaining engines struggled to comply and red lights flared across the panels. The temperature of engine six spiked and another alarm blared from above before Marcus silenced it.

"Six is offline," he said curtly. "Jenny, update?"

"We're here, Marcus." His sister-in-law was out of breath from running through the service halls. "Gia is here. She's okay. Six is a write-off, but I think I can get five back up. Bianca and I are taking the safeties off of the remaining engines to give you a boost. Two minutes, okay?"

"We don't have two minutes, Jenny," Marcus bit out.

Another voice came over the line, tight with strain. "This is Fran. I'm in engine one and I'm about to open up the intake on the coils."

"What? No!" Jenny cried hoarsely. "You'll blow us up!"

"It's our only chance, Mom."

Marcus clutched the edge of the console in front of him, his knuckles white. The two panels on his display showed the pirates closing behind them alongside the *Oro*'s engine output. The empty space where the data from engine four should have been was a black hole, sucking him into the screen.

"Do it, Fran," Marcus said firmly, cutting across Jenny's objections.

Almost immediately the numbers from engine one spiked. Their attackers were still closing, but the rate had dropped.

"Heading to two," Fran called, his footsteps echoing as he ran to the next compartment.

"Jenny, open up the engines on your side," Marcus ordered.

The silence echoed for a moment over the comm, broken only by the shuffling of the children behind him on the bridge.

When Jenny's voice came, it was resolute. "We're on it, Marcus."

"Opening up number two!" Fran called, and the numbers bumped up again, pushing them away from the pirates.

"Opening up number seven now," Jenny said, her voice tight. "It's holding."

"They're all holding," Marcus confirmed. "The pirates are no longer closing."

"I'm opening eight now," Bianca announced. A moment later the distance to closing on the panel increased for the first time.

"We're pulling away!" Marcus shouted, jumping to his feet as cries echoed over the comm and on the bridge behind him.

The exterior comm light flashed and Marcus dropped back down to his seat, shushing everyone.

"This is *Oro* Actual, go ahead, *Sky*."

"*Oro*, I just tightstreamed a file to you. Once you confirm receipt and compliance we will go to radio silence."

Marcus opened the file on this console, reading through it twice before opening the comm again.

"*Sky*, we have received your file." Marcus took a deep breath and swallowed down his fear. "We understand, *Sky*. And we will comply. Thank you."

"What is it?" Cecilia asked, coming to stand over his shoulder. "Why is there...? What? They're going to fire at us?"

Marcus waved her back to her seat. "I'm sending this to your station."

"Marcus!" Cecilia backed toward her seat but stood, hands on hips. "What the hell kind of plan is this?"

He shook his head, rubbing at his tired eyes, and Estelle walked up behind him to place a gentle hand on his shoulder. Marcus took a deep breath. "I don't have a better plan, Cee." He squeezed Estelle's hand and rose to his feet to address the family and crew crowded into the back of the bridge.

Jacob.

Marcus shook his head, pushing back against the grief. There would be time for that later. The *Oro* was a family ship and their highest priority was the children. He ran his eyes over each small face. He thought of them all as his grandchildren, although some were technically his step-grandchildren and his grandnieces and nephews. They all lived aboard this ship as one family–and they would survive this day as one too.

"It's going to be okay," Marcus told them. "Everyone sit down and try to keep quiet, okay? In just a minute we're going to make a big turn."

"Is the other ship going to save us?" asked Jacob's daughter, her brow furrowed like her father's.

"Yes, baby. They're going to save us." Marcus held his smile until he'd turned back to his console and let it fall.

"Marcus?" Cecilia called softly.

He tried to compose his features before turning to her, but her face echoed the fear and pain raging through his chest.

"I've programmed the turn," she said.

There was nothing else they could do now but hold on.

As if spurred by his thoughts, the deck beneath Marcus began to vibrate. Scanning the engine outputs, he opened a channel to engineering, but Jenny's voice cut across the line before he could speak.

"It's engine two!" she cried. "The coils are out of alignment and it's going to blow. I can't shut it down from here."

Marcus opened the panel and initiated the emergency shut-down sequence, the deck beginning to heave beneath him and the children crying out in fear.

"Marcus?" Jenny cried.

"I hear you," he said, "I'm on it." Drilling down through the menus and safeguards, a large red button appeared on the panel and he slapped one hand down on it, the other gripping the edge of the console to keep from being thrown from his chair.

The deck stilled, but Marcus' stomach dropped as the engine output numbers dwindled to zero. They were down another engine. The very people trying to save them might end up destroying the *Oro* if they couldn't turn in time.

"All of you, get up here. We've done all we can."

The deck rocked again and more damage reports rolled across the main screen. The pirates were too far for precise targeting, but they were throwing enough at them to keep getting lucky. The stern of the *Oro* was pitted with near misses. One direct shot and they were dead. One more near miss close enough to an engine, and they were dead. If the pirates didn't get them, they'd run right into their savior's salvo.

"They're gaining on us again, Marcus," Cecilia said softly, her voice resigned.

"I know." Marcus clenched his jaw as the distance between them dwindled. "How long to the turn?"

"Two minutes." Cecilia split the main screen and updated one side with the countdown to the turn. The other side of the screen showed the *Oro* boxed in between their attackers and the red dots of the *Sky*'s missiles.

"Holy crap, they're firing at us!" Harlan cried out from the back of the bridge.

"They're firing at the pirates," Marcus corrected. "We just need to get out of the way."

The remaining members of the crew fell into the bridge. Gia was covered in soot and Harlan held her in his arms as Edward joined them with his med kit. Jenny came to sit beside Cecilia, the two of them gripping hands. Her son, Fran, came and sat at their feet.

Marcus' gaze never left the countdown. The sounds of his family washed over him, faint and far away, as he focused all of his will on the spinning numbers. *Hold on, hold on.*

One by one, the others joined him, staring intently at the countdown. As the bridge fell into silence, the noises of the ship echoed oddly.

Three.

Pings, vibrations, a nerve-chilling grinding tore through the bridge as the *Oro* struggled to move them to safety.

Two.

A faint whine cut through the lower sounds as the ship prepared to turn.

One.

The inertial dampeners struggled to compensate as the huge freighter lurched into its turn and everyone on the bridge scrambled to hold onto something as the ship trembled.

"We're going to make it!" Estelle cried, and an answering call rose up from the family, even as they clung to each other for support.

Their cries of joy were cut off abruptly as the deck dropped out from beneath their feet, sending adults and children alike to the floor. A gut-wrenching groan tore through the bridge, leaving behind silence.

The crew of the *Oro* sat frozen where they'd fallen for a moment, listening intently.

Still in his chair, Marcus shook himself from his daze to check the damage report.

"We're okay, we're okay," he gasped. "It was the aft quarter-panel. It's gone, but we're okay." Marcus ran his hand over his face. "Cecilia, how far are we from the Citadel?"

Her hands shaking, she pulled up the calculations. "If we can hold this velocity, six hours."

"Okay, let's get out of here." Marcus sat back in his chair. His hands were shaking, so he held onto the armrests and took a deep breath. "We made it," he said, as his gaze met Bianca's where she sat on the deck. His son's widow clung to her daughter, and gave Marcus a small nod, before closing her eyes and lowering her head. Estelle moved to sit beside her, wrapping an arm around them both and Marcus was helpless to fight the tears that spilled down his cheeks.

"Oh, no!" Cecilia cried out.

Marcus spun back to the screens as a flare of light winked out where their rescuer's ship had marked the display.

"Are we out of range?" he asked, knuckles white where he gripped his armrests.

Cecilia pulled up the calculations, plotting the pirate's path. "Yes," she gasped out. "We're out of range. They can't catch us before we leave the system."

"Look!" Estelle cried. "The pirates are turning away."

"They're bugging out," Cecilia confirmed.

"Maybe they got off in time," Estelle suggested softly, her hand on her husband's shoulder. "When we get to the station, they'll send back a team to look for survivors."

Marcus nodded, his gaze fixed to the empty spot on the map where the *Sky* had been.

1

Welcome to the Golden Shoe

Maisy passed the rows of unconscious bodies, searching every nook and shadow in the dimly lit bay. The cryobeds were covered with clear domes that glowed from within, the cold white light illuminating each unconscious occupant. Humans were ruled by the illogical urge to *see* with their own eyes. No matter how many blinking lights telegraphed the status of the sleeper, it was the sight of their slack faces that brought comfort to their caretakers. In theory, at least.

"I know you're in here, Joanie," she said gently. Her steps padded softly against the deck as she ventured deeper into the cryobay. This was one of the few sections of the *Oro* that was completely undamaged, but her eyes still skimmed each readout and searched each pale face obsessively.

All indicators green.

Two months into their voyage, the faces were becoming familiar. Old, young. There were twenty-nine members of their rag-tag crew sleeping in this room, riding out the long trip to planet 761 in oblivion. The lucky ones.

As she passed the bank of stacked storage shelves full of frozen genetic material and neared the final cluster of cryobeds, Maisy's steps slowed. They had drawn straws. First for the spots on the emergency pods, then for the cryobeds. Out of the eighty-two passengers remaining on the *Oro*, sixty-five had drawn straws for twenty-six spots in this bay. These last four beds had been reserved for the children.

She searched the small faces for signs of life and tucked a stray curl behind her ear as she checked each panel. Leo's white-blonde hair lay softly against his forehead. There was no movement, no sign of life, but the readouts were all green. His mother Jane spent most of her free time down here, checking on him every day. The boy beside him was Ted, whose parents had died on the Citadel. His panel was green as well.

Maisy's heart squeezed as she laid her fingers gently against the dome of the third chamber. Not yet a year old, Joey's little body, with its shock of bright red hair, was swallowed by the adult-sized cryo unit. His pale lashes rested against his round cheeks and his lips were softly parted, the muscles of his face relaxed. His parents had died in the chaos of their expulsion from the station and sometimes, in her dreams, her own father lay bleeding on the deck beside them. In reality he'd died in space days earlier, but in her mind, the deaths of Joey's parents and that of her father had gotten all jumbled up.

They were all orphans now, but at least Joey still had his sister, Lori. Maisy was grateful that Lori hadn't joined her brother in the cryobay. She couldn't imagine this trip without her, although she wouldn't have blamed her. A year on a patched up freighter, fighting to keep the hull intact and the engines running–who wouldn't want to sleep through that?

When these sleepers woke up, they'd be in a new world. If they made it.

Rustling drew her gaze to the space beneath Joey's unit.

"Hi," she said, crouching down and extending a hand to the little girl tucked into the space.

Joanie allowed Maisy to pull her to her feet and into a hug. She ran a hand over the little girl's closely braided hair and they stood holding each other for a moment. Finally, Maisy sighed and stepped back.

"You can't keep doing this."

Joanie stared her down balefully, with more confidence than any eight-year-old had the right to possess.

Maisy tried again. "You need to accept your mom's decision."

"And how is that going for you?" Joanie shot back.

"That was different!" Maisy protested, waving a hand to encompass their current situation, the bay, the ship, the space station they'd been kicked off of, now several million miles away.

"Was it?" Joanie scoffed with derision. As a teenager herself, Maisy recognized it well.

"For one thing, I was a lot older," she started.

"Not really."

"And my mom had good reasons for her decisions. And not a lot of good options. Just like your mom." Maisy's eyes rested briefly on the last cryo chamber, sitting empty and unused.

Joanie squared her shoulders and folded her arms. "I'm not you. I'm not my mom. I'm making my own decision and I am not going into that thing. Whatever happens between here and planet 761, I'm going to see it."

Joanie met Maisy's gaze firmly, her conviction unwavering. Maisy sighed in defeat.

"Let's go find your mom."

She didn't quite frog march Joanie toward medical, but she kept her within arm's reach as the little girl dragged her feet across the scuffed and worn decking of the hallway. They'd scheduled her cryo induction twice and twice Joanie had pulled this disappearing act. This time there'd been slightly less panic, at least.

Helen, their de facto medical officer, was alone in the medical suite as they entered. She was hunched over a panel, her casted arm resting on the surface, and glanced up with a frown.

"Sue went down to the cafeteria," Helen announced.

"How's the training going?" Maisy asked.

She sighed, sitting back and stretching out her tight shoulders as she repositioned the large cast that ran from mid bicep to palm on her left arm. "It's going. Nobody should break anything else just yet."

"We'll hold off as long as we can," Maisy smiled, ushering Joanie back into the corridor.

When this ship was new the wall panels of the large dining hall had probably been a gleaming white, but now the color was a dingy greige marred by the occasional dent or scratch. As they entered, Maisy's gaze locked onto their usual table, where Lori's red hair was a beacon under the cool LEDs embedded in the room's ceiling.

Sitting across from Lori, Sue tensed and her eyebrows dropped at their appearance and Lori turned to follow her gaze. Sue continued to glower, but Lori's expression softened with relief.

Delaying the inevitable, Maisy led Joanie to the food processors and prepared two plates. They dawdled over the meager selection, but there were only so many ways to prepare plant-based proteins. Maisy haunched her shoulders under the weight of Sue's stare as she finally slid onto the bench. She was grateful when Sue's pointed gaze swung to her daughter.

Joanie picked up her spork and stabbed at one of the batter-fried cubes on her plate, popping it into her mouth. Even her chewing seemed defiant.

Pressing her lips together, Maisy tried to think of a way to bridge the gap. She met Lori's eyes and the other girl gave a slight shake of her head, sending silky red waves sliding over her shoulder.

Swallowing her food, Joanie announced, "We should have another lottery." She scooped up another bite and met her mother's gaze. Sue didn't respond and Joanie continued, "For the last cryobed on the *Golden Shoe*."

"Joanie, we've discussed this," Sue finally bit out. "It's safer for you to ride out the trip in cryo with the boys. Space is a dangerous place."

"Cryo is dangerous, too," Joanie pointed out, dropping her spork onto her plate.

"The *Golden Shoe*?" Lori asked Maisy quietly.

"What if there's an accident?" Sue leaned over the table toward her wayward daughter.

"What if there is?" Joanie replied, sitting on the bench with her back straight and her arms crossed over her chest.

Maisy shrugged at Lori. "The ship. Joanie found a book called *The Golden Shoe* in the classroom and she thinks that's what the ship was named after."

"That is what the ship is named after," Joanie stated firmly. "And what if there's a problem with the cryochamber?"

They all tensed and Sue sat back, her eyes moving to Lori, who frowned. No one wanted to consider that possibility. Cryo tech had been around a long time. Malfunctions were few and far between, but they did happen.

When her mother didn't respond, Joanie pressed on. "What if you have an accident while I'm sleeping and I wake up all alone?"

"You won't be alone," Maisy interjected before she could think better of it. "We're all in it together, no matter what."

"Exactly," Joanie said, staring pointedly at her mother, who cut her eyes toward Maisy.

Impaled by Sue's gaze, Maisy grimaced in apology.

Berta, their de facto captain, moved into the space beside Sue with her own plate. Her gaze swept over the four of them, her expression blank. "I wasn't expecting to see you at dinner, Joanie," she said coolly.

"I'm not going into cryo," Joanie spat back.

Berta's eyes met Maisy's and she shrugged. This was, thankfully, not her battle.

"Have you had a chance to check the roster for tomorrow?" Berta asked, dismissing the other issue as she dug into her dinner.

Uh oh.

"Not yet," Maisy admitted. "What's up?"

"We had to reprioritize the repairs to the lateral struts. Jane's calculations show that they're putting pressure on the hull and that's starting to lower integrity in the forward sections."

"Crap."

"Indeed," Berta concurred. "It's not a problem yet, but it could become one. Tal suggested that the two of you could handle this repair..." She trailed off and quirked an eyebrow.

Maisy nodded, reading between the lines. They certainly weren't going to send Bill, their only pilot, out into the vacuum of space. Berta was their most experienced crew member and equally valuable. Out of the civilians, Maisy had spent the most practice in the suits. And she knew how to weld.

"No problem. We'll handle it."

"I need a job," Joanie announced. "Can Tal teach me to go outside the ship? I could do repairs."

"No," everyone around the table chorused.

After dinner, Lori and Maisy slipped away from the dining room while Sue and Joanie negotiated the terms of surrender.

"Sue never stood a chance," Lori sighed, her green eyes rolling with amusement as a grin pulled up the corner of her lips. Her lashes swept up, longer than her brother's but just as pale.

Maisy nodded in agreement with a rueful smile. "I think Joanie is a great kid." Maisy's smile became a chuckle. "But also kind of terrifying."

Lori burst into laughter and they bumped shoulders as they made their way into the suite they shared with Sue, Joanie, and Jane. They hadn't seen much of Jane since she'd started splitting her time between the cryobay and the bridge.

Crossing to the small kitchen, Lori prepared two coffees and brought them back to the table where Maisy was pulling her tablet out of her bag. Taking the coffee gratefully, Maisy called up the repair list for the next day and compared it to the hydroponics schedule she'd been working on earlier.

There was nothing that couldn't wait.

The *Oro* had been a well-run freighter ship before being shot to hell and the hydroponics bay required minimal maintenance. Among the modern fleets of corporate-leased vessels, it was a throwback to a time when long-haul ships were manned by multi-generational families. From fuel to food, the ship was as self-sufficient as possible. Despite the damage from the *Oro*'s final battle, they were in good shape when it came to supplies—with one notable exception.

Maisy leaned back in her chair to nurse her coffee. Across the table Lori was using a stylus to trace a shape on her own tablet.

"What are you drawing?"

"Nothing," Lori said, then backpedaled. "Well, maybe something." She looked up sheepishly. "I was thinking of painting a mural in the hallway outside of the cafeteria."

"That's a great idea." Maisy's smile tilted up slyly. "I'm sure Joanie would love to help you."

Lori frowned down at her drawing.

"I don't think I want kids," she said abruptly, startling the amusement from Maisy's face.

"But you're so great with Joey." Maisy hesitated and re-grouped. "I just mean..." She gestured vaguely.

Lori shook her head and shrugged, her gaze stuck on the tablet before her. "It's a lot of responsibility."

Maisy nodded, beginning to understand.

"And we're out here in the middle of nowhere with literally no backup plan," Lori continued. "A bunch of kids and burn outs. What's going to happen to us? If we even make it, what does the future look like?"

Lori met Maisy's eyes, her own gaze intense. "For us, for Joey. Will he grow up and be able to have a life? Fall in love someday? Be able to have his own kids?"

"That's a long way off," Maisy said carefully. "I'm really focused on survival right now. I don't think we should start worrying just yet about falling in love. It's not even on my radar," Maisy gave Lori a lopsided smile.

"Yeah, I see that," Lori rolled her eyes.

"What?" Maisy asked, her brow furrowed.

"Nothing. It's okay, Maze." Lori bumped her shoulder against Maisy's. "If I have to be out here, I'm glad I'm out here with you."

"Me too," Maisy settled back into her chair, content.

2

Everything is hard

The spanner floated away into the dark expanse of space and Maisy gritted her teeth. There was no point in lunging for it. The thing was gone. That was the second tool she'd lost this week and they didn't have any to spare. She closed her eyes against the slowly spinning starscape and took a deep breath before opening her comm line.

"Tal, I lost the spanner."

Silence echoed along the line for a long moment. Then came the sound of panting breaths and a bulbous white helmet crested the edge of the *Oro Zapato's* main ion funnel. Tal lumbered into view at a slow, looping jog, mag boots attaching and detaching to the surface of the ship seamlessly.

He rolled to a stop in front of where Maisy was anchored to the forward strut, his smile visible through the clear visor of his faceplate.

"Here you go, Maze." His gloved hand offered another, slightly larger spanner.

She accepted it gingerly. "Aren't you going to yell at me?" She tried to shrug within the stiff suit. "It's not like we have an endless supply of tools. I suck at this."

"I lost way more tools than this when I started and I was almost two years older than you are now," Tal's smile widened. "In fact, you're doing *much* better than I did on my first mission." His smile faltered and he cleared his voice before continuing. "Your dad would be so proud of you."

"My dad would be so proud of himself. He would one hundred percent take credit for any aptitude I may have." She gave Tal a soft punch on the shoulder. "Thanks for the spanner. I promise I won't lose this one."

"No problem, Maze." Accepting that gentle dismissal Tal crossed the surface of the ship back to where he was working, his steps a little slower.

As he disappeared over the edge of the ship, Maisy's eyes searched the star-scattered expanse, trying to imagine the warmth of a thousand distant suns.

With a sigh, she crouched down to apply the tool to the last bolt. When she was satisfied it was tight enough to hold, Maisy carefully tucked the spanner into the pack around her waist and pulled out one of the small welding guns she'd appropriated from the ship's cargo bay weeks ago. The little machines were coming in handy. She polarized her helmet and began sealing the new brace in place with a neat line of molten metal.

"Heading back to you, Maze." Tal's voice jolted her out of the trance she'd entered while working, but her hands remained steady. She finished the line, meeting her starting point.

"I'm done, too." She rose, trying to stretch her sore legs. "I can meet you at the door."

"No!" Tal barked.

Maisy's hand froze.

"No, Maze. Please just wait for me. I'll be right there," he continued in a softer tone.

She moved her hand away from the carabiner anchoring her to the strut as Tal moved across the hull. Silently, she waited for him to reach her.

"Thanks," he smiled, releasing her carabiner and attaching it to his belt. "Let's head back."

Maisy nodded inside her helmet and they started the trek around the port side of the *Oro* to the maintenance airlock. As soon as they reached the door, Tal released the hatch. "After you."

Maisy took a moment to look back over her shoulder at the expanse of space around them. She appreciated the quiet. The interior of the *Oro* was noisy, holding almost double its normal passenger capacity at the moment. She sighed inside her borrowed suit and entered the airlock. The ship's gravity pulled her to the deck and a moment later the outer hatch cut off the view of the stars.

It took several minutes for atmosphere equalization and environmental decontamination scans. By the time they were spat out into the main maintenance bay, she was nearly asleep on her feet. She fumbled with her helmet seal and Tal placed his hands over hers, releasing the catch and lifting the structure from her head.

"Thanks," she mumbled.

"Let's get these suits stowed and then you can hit the hay. You did great out there today, Maze. You really did." Holding onto both helmets, Tal led the way to the suit locker. There were only five functional vacuum-capable suits, which generally caused a small flare of panic in Maisy's chest every time she thought of it. But today she was so tired that the anxiety-inducing reality of having only five functional space suits for the fifty-three people currently walking around the ship barely registered.

"This is hard," she sighed, sinking to the deck and struggling out of the reinforced plates and plastisteel maille. Tal shimmied out of his suit with insulting dexterity and then held the shoulders of her suit while she flopped about like a demented butterfly breaking free from her shiny white cocoon.

Finally, her last leg emerged unscathed. Tal tucked the pieces of the suit into their decon locker while Maisy sprawled on the floor in her underwear, panting.

"It's always going to be hard," she said to the ceiling. "From now on."

Tal finished putting the last pieces of his own suit away and crouched down beside her on the deck. He didn't say anything and Maisy turned her head to look at him. His face was angled down, his eyes staring at an empty spot on the deck, and Maisy instantly regretted saying anything.

An alarm sounded from above and a red flashing light flooded the room. Maisy launched herself off the floor and reached for the wrist unit she'd left sitting on top of the locker. Slapping it on, she opened a line to the bridge.

"Jane!" she yelled into the unit, pulling on clothes. "What's going on?"

"Um, this is Gary," replied a tentative voice. "Jane isn't on the bridge."

"Where's Berta?"

"She's fixing a problem down in bay twelve. It's just me here," he stuttered.

"Gary, what's going on?" Maisy kept her voice even as she slipped on her shoes.

"So, um, it looks like it's engine number five again. The system is saying that the temp is too high and it's going to need a manual shutdown." Gary finished reading the alert, panting as if he'd just completed a marathon.

"Ok. Tal and I are headed that way. Go ahead and turn off the alarm, please."

"Turn off the alarm...gotcha."

As Gary's voice faded away, Maisy closed the line and took off for the engineering deck, Tal hot on her heels.

The alarm followed them from the maintenance bay, across the ship, down two levels, and was still blaring when they made it to engine room five. Maisy was about to call back to the bridge when it finally cut off. Her wrist unit binged.

"Maisy?" came Jane's familiar voice into the silence.

"We're here," Maisy gasped, slightly out of breath from the run across the ship. "We're shutting down number five."

"I'm starting the sequence," Tal called from across the room at the main panel.

"Tal is starting the manual shutdown now," Maisy relayed. She opened the coolant analysis on the maintenance panel and scrolled through the most recent logs. "What the hell?"

"What?" Tal asked without glancing up from his task. The faint hum of the engine changed tones.

Maisy tapped through the data again, confirming her conclusions. "It looks like there's debris in the coolant." She glanced over at Tal, her mind racing with the implications. "It's contaminated."

"What?" This time Tal glanced up. "No way. We were so careful."

"Not careful enough. There are clogged injectors and the flow was reduced by 20% over the last twelve hours." Maisy took a step back from the console and braced her hands on her hips, trying to control her breathing. There had been eight engines on the *Oro*. Number four had been completely destroyed in the pirate's attack, number two was stubbornly offline, and they'd been babying number six along so far. Number five was the thorn in their side.

"We can't lose this engine again," Tal muttered, shutting down the engine. "We just can't. The passengers will riot if we lose more time. Where the hell are we going to find more coolant?"

"We'll–" Another alarm sounded, cutting Maisy off. They both raised their heads, waiting for it to die again. When it didn't, Maisy ran for the elevator, Tal at her side.

"What now?" he muttered as they approached the bridge.

The alarm abruptly cut off, leaving behind the sound of strident voices.

"We're going to wait for them to get here before we make any decisions," Jane said firmly.

"You know they're just a couple of kids, right?" Bill, the pilot, asked. "What is she, like sixteen?"

Maisy entered the bridge to find Jane facing off with the much shorter man, toe to toe. Gary sat at engineering, his eyes bouncing between the two.

"And you're just a former marine who may or may not still work for an evil conglomerate that tried to send a bunch of innocent people to their deaths for the sake of profit and expediency." Jane crossed her arms and leaned back to look down her nose. "So let's just wait until Maisy and Tal get back to make any decisions. Right, Bill?"

"We're here," Tal announced. "Number five is shut down. What's going on now?"

Jane moved to the navigation workstation and Maisy crossed the bridge to stand at her side.

"There's a ship," Jane announced, nodding at the display.

"Out here?" Tal's voice rose in shock.

"How did it get so close before we detected it?" Maisy asked, her eyes on the panel. "Any ID?"

Bill spoke up from behind them. "We couldn't come up with anything. They're completely offline."

"Let me see," Tal mumbled, already engrossed in the data coming up on the telemetry console. "It's only 5000 metric tons, so not a freighter." He changed the settings on the array. "No heat signatures. Maybe emergency power, but I don't see it." He swiped the data up and glanced at the main bridge display. "Here's a visual."

"Pirate attack?" Berta asked from the doorway to the bridge. She walked across the deck and they all examined the image on the screen.

Maisy's blood ran cold at the large hole in the rear of the ship.

"I don't think so," Tal answered. "See the tearing around the edges? That looks like a blown engine."

"There were two alarms?" Berta raised a brow.

"Engine five," Tal mumbled, manipulating the image of the derelict vessel on his screen.

"Again?" Berta sighed, dropping into the captain's chair. "You've got to be kidding me."

The vessel rotated on its long axis. Maisy leaned forward, tapping the panel on the console before her to zoom in and enhance the image.

"There's a hull number," she said. The ship continued to spin, revealing lettering. "The Kittredge," Maisy read.

"Got it!" Tal moved a profile onto the other side of the big screen. "She's a Suki-Nyberg ship. Registered as a science vessel."

"Did any coolant survive that blast?" Maisy wondered out loud.

Tal clapped his hands together. "Only one way to find out."

***

"Everything is okay." Maisy leaned a hip against the cafeteria table and nursed her coffee as she considered the people before her.

"What was the alarm this time? Where is the captain?" asked an older man, his beard peppered with white.

Another man leaned forward. "Is it the engine again?" His voice broke. "Is life support ok?"

"The ship is okay!" Maisy assured them, waving a hand. "Tal and I completed the repairs on the array and that issue is resolved." Maisy gestured vaguely at the ceiling. "There were two separate alarms. The first one was about the coolant issue with engine five. The second alarm was a proximity sensor."

The older man paled. "We hit something?"

"No! Everything is fine, Curtis, I swear," Maisy rushed to assure him, but he shook her off.

"Why isn't the captain talking to us?"

Maisy sighed. *Good question.* "You know Berta doesn't want to be called captain, Curtis."

"She's the senior officer!" he protested.

"They're not marines, man," the other passenger sneered. "They're Security Services, just like the goons that put us on this death trap."

"That's not fair, Loy," Maisy began, but was drowned out by other questions.

"So what tripped the sensor?"

"There's something out there?"

Maisy raised her hand until they quieted down.

"There's another ship," she told them.

Curtis raised bushy eyebrows. "Out here?" The *Oro* was well past the outer sensors and months from any regular shipping lanes.

"Yeah, it looks abandoned and it's pretty badly damaged."

"Damaged?" Loy cut in. "Like another pirate attack?"

"We don't think so," Maisy answered. "Some kind of malfunction, maybe. It's a science vessel, so who knows what it was doing out here. It's not a Citatech ship so it shouldn't have been in this quadrant at all," Maisy shrugged. "It's drifting and it looks like nobody's home, but we're going to put together a team to go over and check it out." Maisy cast her gaze out over the assembled crowd. She needed an extra set of hands, or two.

"Is anyone interested in going with us? I'd like to have at least a couple more bodies."

The crowd began to disperse, but a young man from the back moved up.

"I'll go." He looked over his shoulder and waved his brother forward. "Paulie will come too."

Paulie was shorter and rounder but had the same sandy hair and blue eyes as his brother. "Yup! I'm in."

"Great. I'm hoping there might be supplies to bring back. We really need coolant, and I'd love to grab some medical supplies."

"Lucas and I are happy to help, Maze," Paulie assured her.

"Thanks, guys," Maisy nodded at her two volunteers. "Let's meet in the maintenance bay in thirty minutes."

Maisy refilled her coffee and hurried from the cafeteria. Hydroponics was two levels up and she needed to check the moisture levels before leaving the ship.

"Maisy."

She stopped short and frowned as a drop fell from the rim of her over-full cup. It was going to be a long day and she needed every bit of caffeine she could get.

"What is it, Bill?" As grateful as Maisy had been when the pilot decided to stay with the *Oro* rather than returning to the Citadel with his psychopathic captain, she was short on time and patience.

Bill hesitated at her tone, but forced himself to carry on. "Are you going with the away team?"

Maisy narrowed her eyes. "Do you have a problem with me?"

Bill flinched. "No," he said earnestly. "I just thought someone...older...would be doing this."

Fighting hard not to roll her eyes, Maisy forced a smile. "Tal will be leading the team. I won't be unsupervised."

"It isn't that, Maisy," he insisted. "I just think you're way too young to have this much responsibility on your shoulders."

"Then take some of it," she responded.

Bill's eyes widened and his mouth flopped open but no words emerged.

"I know it would be too much of a risk to send our only pilot onto a derelict ship, but I've got a list as long as my arm," she continued aggressively. "What part would you like to take on? Food? Medical? Repairs? There are a lot of people on this ship..." Maisy sighed, the long day catching up with her again.

When she started speaking again, her tone was quieter and her shoulders sagged. "And a lot of them just seem to be along for the ride."

They stared at each other in silence for a moment.

Finally Maisy shook her head and shrugged. "I know I'm not the right person. None of us are—but there's no one else here. So I'm open to suggestion, Bill. If there's someone else who would do a better job, just let me know." With that she walked away.

In hydroponics, Maisy checked the control panel and visually examined each tank. Like the engines, hydroponics was basically a closed system with four components. The bacteria level was flourishing, as usual. The plants looked good. Maisy placed a hand against the glass of the shrimp tank, relieved to find it teeming with life.

The fourth component of the cycle was the human factor, of course. From the records they'd found, the *Oro* had run for decades with a crew of about 30. Removing that crew entirely and leaving the ship empty for several days–and then throwing 113 people into the environment had nearly killed off the entire ecosystem. The first thing to bounce back was the bacteria plumes, but different people produced different bacteria and it had been touch and go for a few days.

But now, the bright, humid room was awash in greens and reds and tiny shrimp swam up to touch the glass where Maisy's fingers rested against it. The various types of algae had adapted to the new bacteria mix, and the shrimp would pretty much eat anything. They'd be happy to nibble her fingers if she let them.

Between the algae and the shrimp, the food processors in the cafeteria could make an impressive variety of meals. They'd been careful not to over-harvest the first couple of weeks on board, but now that the cryosleepers were out of the loop, it seemed like they'd hit the sweet spot.

Content that their food source was bobbing along happily, Maisy headed to the maintenance bay.

3

The Ghost

Tal spun the manual hatch wrench one more rotation and the airlock on the *Kittridge* popped open with a sigh.

"We've got atmo," he panted, hooking the glorified crowbar to his belt. "And gravity. Let's see what else is in here." Using the hand holds built into the sides of the airlock, Tal pulled himself through the opening and made contact with the decking. Maisy and the two brothers were right on his heels, the four of them tethered together.

The headlamps on each suit's helmet illuminated the airlock as they crowded into the small space. Tal opened a panel beside the interior hatch to reveal a large lever, sized for gloved hands.

"Ok, Maze. Go ahead and close the outer hatch."

"Got it," Maisy replied, pulling the heavy door. Gripping the lever she pistoned it until the gap closed and the airlock was once again sealed. Arm aching, Maisy finally stepped back and gave Tal a thumbs up.

Nodding, he pumped the manual lever until the interior door opened with a sigh.

"Okay, let's see what we can see," Tal muttered as he ducked into darkness.

Lucas and Paulie hesitated, so Maisy pushed past them and into the ghost ship. Tugging on the tether, she waited impatiently while the brothers followed her inside.

"Wow. This is just like *Orion 5*," Paulie gasped.

Maisy glanced back at him. "What's that?" A memory sparked and she frowned. "Is that the game you guys have been playing on the network?"

Paulie smiled sheepishly. "Yeah. It's an oldie but a goodie."

Maisy tried hard not to roll her eyes and followed the lights of Tal's suite to where he dug inside an electrical panel.

"There's power," he muttered. "Looks like everything was just shut down."

"That's good news, right?" Maisy stared into the mess of wires Tal was prodding but couldn't make heads or tails of it.

"Yeah, that's great news. It will make our job much easier." Pulling a small tablet from his toolbelt, he extended a line into the panel and made a connection.

"Can you get into the system?" Maisy asked, impressed.

"Not from here. But if I can just ping the lights, it will make getting around a lot easier." He entered a command on the tablet and their surroundings were bathed in light. It was a large maintenance bay, not unlike the one on the *Oro*.

"There we go!" Tal unhooked his tablet and placed it back into his belt before turning to Maisy and the brothers.

"Hey Paulie, see if that hatch button works now."

With a swoosh the interior hatch to the airlock slid shut and Tal reached up to release his helmet.

"The system is likely intact, since the lights responded to the standard wake up command. If we can get onto the bridge, I should be able to run a full diagnostic and get some more info."

Maisy nodded, pulling off her own helmet and letting it fall back and dangle against her shoulders. "It will be good to have the data, but our primary goal is to scavenge what we can."

"We need coolant, and any engine parts they have," Tal agreed.

"And food," Paulie offered as he and his brother removed their helmets. "Wow, it's cold in here."

Maisy shrugged. "We're lucky there's air. We're actually in pretty good shape when it comes to food, but yeah, we'll take what we can get." She grimaced. "But our first priority is engineering. Without coolant we're never getting engine five online again."

"Let's split up to cover more ground–"

Maisy cut Tal off and squeezed the arm of his suit with her gloved hand. "No. We stick together. We'll head to the bridge first, okay?"

"Okay, Maze." Tal reached across and covered Maisy's hand. "We'll stick together."

"This is a touching moment and all, but can we at least untether?" Paulie grunted as Lucas bopped the back of his head with his gloved hand, but Maisy laughed and showed the younger brother how to unclip his carabiner.

"Just stay close, okay?"

"Absolutely."

The hallways were bright, but covered in a layer of crystallized dust. They echoed oddly the way spaces made for people do when they're completely empty. On earth there were still places where one could imagine no human had ever set foot. There the silence was peaceful and comforting. Here it was creepy.

Maisy and Tal shared a look when they reached the bridge to find the hatch standing open.

"Interesting," Tal muttered as he tapped into the main engineering console.

"Do you think you can get in?" Maisy came up to stand at his shoulder. On the panel before them system status indicators scrolled past, half red.

"I'm already in," he waved at the screen. "Everything is wide open."

"That's weird, isn't it?" Lucas asked, joining them.

The four of them crowded around the panel as Tal filtered down into the system to find the most recent logs.

"Okay...looks like the engine was experimental and it blew. After that the environmental system went into a shutdown and they had to abandon ship."

"Environmentals?" Maisy echoed. "But it's okay now?"

Tal tapped at the control panel built into the left arm of his suit. "Yeah, the air quality is totally fine." He went back to the panel and pulled up the system's diagnostics on the screen. "The whole system is green."

"What kind of engine was it? Will they still have the coolant we need for the *Oro*?"

"They should. Let's see if I can get into their inventory. Anything in the engine compartment most likely was vented in the explosion." Tal tapped for a moment. "Yes! Looks like they have plenty. It's in storage bay two. Wow, this must have been a really long mission. Look at how well stocked this ship was."

"Let's grab it and head back. We can come back over tomorrow."

"Okay. I'm in the network, so I'll be able to go through their logs and inventory from the *Oro*."

Traipsing back down the hallway, they passed the maintenance bay to a large storage bay. Again the door was standing open for them and Maisy frowned as they passed through the hatch.

In the middle of the room, two pallets of ion stable coolant were stacked neatly onto a hover cart.

***

Maisy tapped the face of her wrist unit to turn off the alarm without opening her eyes. The lights were programmed to brighten gradually as ship's dawn approached and she knew the room would be softly illuminated. But for a moment she laid quietly in the bed, listening to the noises around her.

When they'd first arrived on the *Oro*, it had been a tight fit and everyone had double and tripled-up. Maisy and her friends had grabbed this three bedroom suite that first day. It was probably four times the size of the unit Maisy had shared with her father on the station, so none of them had complained. Now, of course, Joey and Leo were in the cryobay.

Maisy rolled over and opened her eyes to search Lori's sleeping face. It had made sense to prioritize the kids for the cryochambers. Space was a dangerous place, and not an ideal environment for a baby under any circumstances.

Lori's golden brown eyelashes fluttered and Maisy held very still, trying not to wake her. After a moment, Lori rolled onto her back and stretched, groaning. Her morning process was more gradual.

By the time Lori seemed semi-conscious and had rolled back to face her, Maisy was smiling.

"Good morning."

"Absolutely not," Lori countered firmly.

Maisy chuckled, snuggling down into the bed a little more. There was so much to do, but they had a little time.

"What's on your list for today?"

"Not all of us wake up like cats, you know," Lori snarked, rolling her eyes. "I don't even know my own name yet, much less what day it is or what I'm going to be doing hours from now."

"Your name is Lori," Maisy snickered softly. "And I'm pretty sure I know the first thing on your list."

"And what's that, Miss Know-It-All?"

"Coffee!" Maisy crowed, right before the pillow hit her in the face.

Half an hour later, Maisy was scrolling through the inventory of the *Kittridge* as Lori savored her last drop of coffee. Lowering her cup, she met Maisy's eyes across the table.

"You may speak to me now."

Maisy grinned. "Welcome back to the land of the living, Sunshine."

"Be gentle, the caffeine is still percolating through my veins." Lori reached out and poked at Maisy's tablet with a finger. "Anything good in there?"

"Yeah, it's quite the haul. Lots of supplies, spare parts, tools."

Lori leaned forward and lowered her voice. "Have you heard the rumor?"

"Rumor? About what?"

"Aliens," interrupted a dry voice from the far end of the suite. Jane emerged from her bedroom, running a hand through her short blonde hair.

Lori sat back, giggling at Maisy's expression.

"Seriously?" Maisy asked. "Who started that one? Lucas or Paulie?" She rolled her eyes and lifted her own coffee cup to take a sip.

"I'm pretty sure Lucas started the alien rumor and Paulie started the ghost rumor," Lori answered as Jane joined them at the table.

"To be honest, it was kind of creepy," Maisy shrugged.

The door buzzed. After a moment, Lori jumped up and crossed to unlock the panel. It slid open to reveal Tal, an uncharacteristic frown on his lean face.

"What's up?" Maisy asked in concern.

Tal crossed to join them at the table, Lori on his heels. "Have you taken a look at the engine configuration on the *Kittridge*?" He waved at the tablet in his hand.

Maisy had access to all of the data, but she'd only focused on the inventory. "No, what's wrong with it? Besides the fact that it blew up."

"Was it built by aliens?" Jane asked with a smile.

Tal did a double take. "What?"

"That's the story floating around," she explained. "Or at least one of them."

Tal shook his head, staring down at the blank screen of the tablet in his hands.

"There have always been rumors, of course," he said quietly, almost to himself.

"About aliens?" Joanie asked from the door of the bedroom she shared with her mother. Sue appeared behind her a moment later and they both headed straight for the small kitchen.

"Lucas is telling everyone there's alien tech on the ghost ship," Joanie announced as she poured her own cereal.

Tal's lips twisted in a grimace and he looked helplessly at Maisy.

"What's wrong?" she asked.

Tal pulled up a schematic on his tablet and slid it across the table to her. "Look at that configuration."

She picked up the tablet and zoomed into the engine design displayed. "It's not a coil."

"No, it's not."

Jane held out a hand to Maisy, who passed over the tablet. "Is it some kind of new tech?" Jane manipulated the image. "I've never seen anything like this in twenty years of engineering."

"Something experimental?" Maisy asked.

"You wouldn't put an experimental engine on a ship that size. If it had been around long enough to get to that point, I'd have seen something." Jane shook her head, zooming into different views of the engines. "It doesn't make sense."

"It did blow up," Maisy pointed out. She looked at Tal consideringly. "You don't really think this is some kind of alien tech, do you?"

"There have always been rumors," he said again.

Maisy sat back from the table, frowning. "You can't be serious."

"Listen, this ship was built by Suki-Nyberg, and SN comes up with off the wall stuff all the time. They don't play by the rules." Tal hesitated. "Your dad was pretty sure they were behind the pirate attacks."

"The pirates? The ones who shot up the *Oro*? The ones who..." Maisy let her voice trail off. *The ones who killed my dad.*

"The ones who destroyed the *Sky*," Tal said. He sighed and gestured toward the tablet still in Jane's hands. "This isn't next gen."

"No," Jane agreed, handing back the tablet. "It's a completely new line of engineering."

"So if you think this is alien tech–" Lori started.

"Or derived from alien tech," Tal pointed out.

"--where did it come from? Could Suki-Nyberg be trading with an alien species out here?"

"Is that why the corporate violence has escalated in the last year?" Maisy wondered out loud.

"SN trying to protect their new resource?" Jane added.

"Could that be why Citatech didn't send a real colony ship to 761?" Lori asked.

Tal shook his head. "I have no idea...but it would have been really good to know that before now."

"Does it really change anything?" Maisy asked.

"Well, yeah. If there is hostile sentient life out here–"

Lori cut Tal off. "They can't be too hostile if they're trading with one of the corporations."

Tal shrugged. "Well, I guess that's true."

"Let's hope so. We have enough problems without adding hostile alien lifeforms to the mix." She rolled her eyes. "There should be more info in their systems. We'll figure it out. There must be a reasonable explanation."

"It's definitely aliens," Joanie announced around a mouthful of cereal.

4

The enemy you know

The spectrometer beeped as the readout appeared on the main engineering panel. Tal rose from where he was crouched beside a case of coolant to read the results and let out the breath he'd been holding with a whoop.

"We're in business," he crowed, smiling at Maisy where she sat at a station, pouring over the schematics for engine five.

"Excellent." Maisy sent her current view to Tal's display. "Take a look at this." She stood and walked over to join him.

"See this area? With the bifurcated node? It doesn't match up to the actual ion lattice anymore." Maisy tapped the screen to zoom into the changed area on the schematic. "This is where the coolant became contaminated. Someone must have repaired this engine on the fly and they just spliced this section. It even could have happened during the pirate attack"

"That makes sense." Tal gripped the edge of the panel. "It was a nasty fight. The *Oro* was desperate to pour on as much acceleration as possible while the pirate's weapons ate away at their stern."

"This is probably why number five overheated in the first place," Maisy mused. "And why all of our fixes haven't worked."

Tal ran a hand through his shock of thick brown hair, which sprang back up immediately. "And why we've just been wasting coolant. If not for the *Kittridge*, we'd be in real trouble." Tal shook off his mood and transferred the schematic to his tab. He turned to Maisy with a smile, looking much more like himself. "Want to help me tear apart this junction and completely rebuild it so we can get this baby back up and running?"

An hour later Maisy was silently cursing herself for saying yes. The reason for the contamination at the re-spliced junction had become obvious the longer they worked on it. There wasn't enough room to get their tools into the space to properly seal the weld.

"Crap!" Maisy reared back as she cracked another knuckle. Sticking the offended appendage into her mouth, she sucked on it until the worst of the pain had passed.

Pulling her torso from the maintenance panel, Maisy slumped onto the catwalk and eyed Tal's lanky body. There was no point in complaining. Even though his arms were longer, Tal's shoulders were too wide to get him close enough to make the repair. Maisy looked at her hands, now covered in knicks and red marks and sighed.

"I'm sorry, Maze."

"It's not your fault," Maisy gave a half-hearted smile. "Give me a minute and I'll try again."

Resting back against the wall of the engine housing, Maisy flexed her fingers as she let her thoughts wander.

"I didn't know that the pirates were from Suki-Nyberg," she said finally, her eyes on her battered hands.

"All of the corporations fund them, really," he said. "The ones from SN seem a little more brutal than the rest, but they've all been pretty bad this past year."

"Even Citatech?"

"I'm sure they do," Tal nodded. "We wouldn't have heard about it on the Citadel because of the censors. Since the coalition pulled out it's just gotten a lot worse."

"How did you know it was SN who attacked the *Oro*?"

"We were able to ID the ship. The *Penny Farthing*." Tal closed his eyes. "Your dad didn't seem surprised at all."

"That the pirates were SN?"

Tal nodded without opening his eyes. "It was the missiles." His eyes opened but his gaze was still somewhere far away, and months ago. "I'm not sure what happened, but the new missiles we were testing were from SN. The specs were all just a little off. I couldn't figure it out." Tal's eyes finally moved to Maisy's. "But Jackson saw it right away."

Maisy's brow furrowed as her jaw tightened. "It was some kind of setup?"

"I don't know," Tal said, his voice soft and strained.

"Did Citatech set them up? My dad? The *Oro*?"

"I don't know." Tal sighed. "This is why I haven't said anything before. I just don't know. And all of the evidence is gone."

Maisy leaned forward, her eyes hard. "Tell me exactly what you remember."

***

Maisy leaned against the side of the elevator, cradling her hand to catch the droplets of blood before they could fall to the metal decking. There were bots to clean the floors, but if they'd been sufficient to take care of a crew of thirty, they were having a hard time keeping up with fifty-three. Chances were if she bled on the deck, she'd be the one to have to clean it up.

The doors opened and Maisy stumbled down the hallway toward the open hatch of medical. Inside Helen sat at the console, watching another training vid with a suture kit open on the table before her. Her partner Sean was stretched out on one of the beds, tablet in hand and a game on the screen.

"Hey, Helen. Ready to practice with the regen wand?" Maisy forced a smile as Helen jumped up and hustled over to her side.

"What have you done now?" she scolded, ushering Maisy toward the beds.

Sean lurched up with wide eyes. "I'll get out of your way," he mumbled as he made a beeline for the door.

Helen bit off a reply as he passed and focused back on her patient.

After helping Maisy hoist herself onto the empty bed, she ran her uncasted hand under the decom field beside the sink and pulled a new wound kit from the cabinet. One-handed, she broke the seal and extracted the sterile mat. Lying it across Maisy's lap, she gently pulled Maisy's hands apart to see the damage.

"I was trying to fix engine five and my hand slipped," Maisy said, gritting her teeth as Helen gently prodded the charred gash across her hand.

Helen clucked her tongue. "Infection and pain management are our primary concerns with burns," she recited. "So we'll clean the wound, give it a pass with the wand, and then seal it, right?"

Maisy nodded stiffly, "Sounds good to me."

The antiseptic in the kit included an analgesic, so Maisy was more relaxed by the time Helen started working with the wand.

"The bleeding has stopped, but this isn't working as well as I thought it would on the burned area," she muttered. "Hold on for a minute, Maze. I'll be right back." Helen ran over to the console and tapped through the med tutorials. "Ah ha. Burn wounds need to be debrided before using the regen wand. Okay, got it."

Maisy kept herself from flinching and smiled encouragingly as Helen pulled out a small spray bottle.

"This is the enzymatic debrider. It should only take a couple of seconds to clear out the damaged tissue and then we'll hit it again with the wand." Helen pumped the spray twice and Maisy's arm lit up with pain.

"Stop!" She panted. "It burns! Something's wrong." Maisy gripped her wrist as if she could stop the pain running up her arm if she squeezed hard enough. "Wash it off! Wash it off, Helen!"

"Wait! Hold on, Maze. Breathe with me. It's working. It should just take a minute." Helen put her hand over the one around Maisy's wrist and held the injured hand in place while she squirmed against the pain.

As Maisy was about to leap up and put it under the tap herself, the pain faded. It fell away like it had never been there, leaving Maisy drained.

"It's better now," She said limply.

Helen pressed her hand to Maisy's cheek. "I'm so sorry, Maze." She patted her shoulder, and picked up the wand again. "I had no idea it would hurt like that or I would have warned you."

She ran the wand over the injury and this time the edges disappeared, blending together as the wound granulated in and the color evened out.

Maisy's breathing returned to normal, her body sagging. "I need a nap," she said, trying not to slur her words.

"Yes, you do," Helen agreed. She placed a clear adhesive film over the wound and held an injector to Maisy's skin. Maisy didn't even flinch.

Helen gathered her supplies and put them into the recycling station and returned to stand over Maisy for a moment, her forehead creased in worry.

"That shot should put you out for a couple of hours, but when you wake up you'll feel better."

***

Maisy woke up alone, with no sense of place or time. She was on the *Oro*, but Lori wasn't beside her. Maisy always woke up first. Where was Lori?

As she pushed herself up from the bed her hand hit the mattress. It didn't hurt but the skin pulled tight against muscle and bone. The bandage gave her skin a plastic sheen and sparked the memory of the burn and going to Helen in medical. She remembered the searing pain of the spray.

It was nearly 6pm, the time the inhabitants of the *Oro* assembled each day to compare notes and get in some socialization, but Maisy was groggy and wanted nothing more than to roll over and head back to sleep. She sat for a moment on the edge of the bed, willing herself to get up.

"Maze?"

Lori stood in the doorway to their bedroom, her eyes darkened with concern.

"Helen sent me to check on you. How are you feeling?" Lori crossed the room to sit beside Maisy on the bed. She reached out to place a hand on her forehead, her lips tightening at the clamminess on Maisy's skin.

Shrugging her off, Maisy pushed to her feet. "I'm okay. Give me two minutes in the bathroom and I'll be ready for dinner."

True to her word, soon the two were making their way to the cafeteria. Maisy ignored Lori's concerned glances, straightening her back and trying to walk smoothly.

"I'm fine," she cut her gaze to Lori, who hummed in response. "Seriously," Maisy insisted.

"Okay, I believe you," Lori lied as they entered the mess hall.

Maisy was frowning intently at Lori when Tal swooped in from her other side to pull her into a one-armed hug.

"Dear god, I swear I'm fine," she bit out, struggling from the embrace.

Tal held onto her shoulders, but let her step back enough that he could see her face. Reaching for her hand, he pulled it close to examine the remains of the wound.

"See?" Maisy asked.

"This looks good," Tal squinted at Helen's work. "I was so worried. I checked in with Helen as soon as the ion assembly was back together but she said she'd sent you to rest and I shouldn't bug you."

Maisy pulled back her hand and waved his concerns away. "She did a great job. I'm good as new." Moving forward between Tal and Lori, she headed toward the food processors.

"Have you eaten yet?" she asked over her shoulder.

Tal followed in her wake. "No, I was waiting for Lori to come back with you." He snagged her shoulder and redirected her to their usual table. "You guys go sit down. I'll bring back three plates."

Lori and Tal shared a significant look and Lori bumped Maisy's shoulder to move her along. Sue caught her eye, waving her over insistently, and Maisy sighed, succumbing to the inevitable, and let herself be herded to their table.

Since their arrival on the *Oro*, their small group had maintained the tradition of eating together in the cafeteria every evening and encouraged the rest of the crew to do so as well. At this point everyone had a tablet or wrist unit to get updates, but meeting in person at least once a day meant they were getting to know each other. Depending on the repairs to engine five, the voyage to 761 could take a year, or more. That was way too long for the passengers to sit in their rooms playing games.

Maisy pushed that thought away as she maneuvered herself gingerly onto the bench, startling when Helen plopped down beside her, resting her casted arm on the table. Sighing, Maisy offered her hand obediently and sat quietly as Helen examined her handiwork.

"This is looking good, Maze," she said as she finally released Maisy's hand back to its owner.

"It feels a lot better."

"I'm so sorry about the enzyme spray. I had no idea it stung like that. I looked it up after you left and I should have used the separate analgesic in the blue bottle. The one in the antiseptic isn't strong enough." Helen's voice was firm and clear but her face was pale and there were lines of tension around her eyes.

"It really is okay," Maisy said, reaching out to touch the back of her hand. "I'd much rather find out on me than on someone else. You're doing great."

"I have a lot to learn," Helen sighed.

"We all do," Maisy shrugged.

5
Winners and losers

"Well, look who decided to join us," Sue muttered under her breath.

Joanie had joined Tal at the food processors and a moment later the two headed to the table side by side. Tal handed off one of the plates he was juggling and the little girl bopped her way across the room, miraculously spilling nothing.

"Hi, Maisy!" Joanie said, sliding the plates onto the table. "Here's your dinner. Tal said you got hurt today." Joanie swung onto the bench and shoveled a square of synthetic protein-enriched cornbread into her mouth and continued to talk around it. "Can I see your hand?"

Maisy once again put up no resistance as her hand was inspected, this time with a touch of disappointment.

"Hmmm. You can't see any blood or bone or anything," Joanie complained.

Maisy smiled. "Well, that's because Helen did such a good job."

"Hmmm," Joanie said again, as her mother rolled her eyes.

"And where were you all day, madam?" Sue asked. The two frowned at each other wearing matching expressions.

Maisy's heart tightened for a moment. "You guys are so alike," she sighed, and matching sherry brown eyes turned her way. "It's kind of awesome when you look just like your mom," Maisy told Joanie.

"Do you look like your mom?" she asked, head cocked.

"Yeah," Maisy gave her a sad smile.

Joanie frowned, gears turning, then glanced back at her mother. "We're staying together, right? You're not still going to try to put me into a cryochamber?"

Sue searched her daughter's face, her own expression softening. "Yes, Baby, we're staying together." Sue reached across the table to pat Maisy's hand again. "All of us."

"Yay!" Joanie reached out and slapped her hand over her mother's.

"I'm in, too," Lori smiled at the happy faces around the table and placed her hand over Joanie's.

"Can I be in?" Tal asked sheepishly.

Joanie beamed at him. "Yes!"

His hand joined the pile.

"And Jane too!" Joanie announced.

Maisy nodded. "She's on the bridge, but absolutely yes, Jane too. Can I have my hand back now?"

Joanie fell into a fit of giggles as they all sat back in their seats and began eating their dinners. Joanie's meal was heavy on the cornbread and Maisy was happy to find a little more variety on her own plate. Her hunger had snuck up on her and everyone ate in silence for a moment.

Once she'd hoovered her plate, Joanie put her elbows on the table and leaned forward earnestly. "We need to hold a raffle," she announced.

Her mother looked at her blankly.

"For the last cryo," she explained, drawing out the syllables.

Sue gave a deep sigh and looked to Maisy, who shrugged.

"Okay, Joanie. We'll raffle off the last spot. Do you want to go get the straws?"

Joanie was up and running across the cafeteria before Sue finished her sentence. "We're raffling off another cryo spot!" she yelled as she went.

The conversation level in the room ramped up and Maisy looked around, trying to note who wasn't present. Jane and Bill were on the bridge. Berta, the other former marine on board was also missing. Like Tal, Bill and Berta had been given the chance to take one of the escape pods before the *Oro* exited the busy shipping lanes. Jane had made her decision to help with the voyage–she was one of the few passengers with real technical skills.

At this point Maisy knew the rest of the passengers on the *Oro* by name, but besides the people at her table, their stories were largely still a mystery. She assumed they were similar to her own. They'd been removed from the Citadel and told they had no choice except to join a colony ship–which turned out to be a derelict freighter with extensive battle damage. It was the *why*, that differed in each case.

Maisy had been the dependent of a marine killed in duty. She had no purpose on the Citadel, an ore processing station built into the side of an asteroid. Lori's parents had been valuable workers–but her mom ran the local union. Station management had weighed her value versus the trouble she caused and the scales had not tipped in her favor. They'd been killed resisting their forced expulsion from the station.

Once the coalition government had pulled out of the quadrant, the corporations had wasted no time casting off the reins of the rule of law. They didn't have anyone to force them to tolerate the unions, so they didn't. They also didn't need safety inspectors, which was how Sue found herself on the *Oro*.

Joanie came running back up with a fist full of straws and an entourage.

"Lucas?" Maisy raised her eyebrows. "Are you joining the raffle this time?" The brothers had sat out the last raffle, seeming to embrace the adventure of the voyage. She couldn't imagine them opting for cryo now, especially if it meant them splitting up.

"Nah, not me, Maze," he answered with a chuckle. "I'm just here to catch the deathmatch."

"Hopefully it isn't going to be that entertaining," Maisy muttered. There had been some hard feelings last time, but no one had come to blows.

Joanie dropped the straws onto the table before Maisy and addressed the crowd she'd drawn. "Raise your hand if you want to draw!" she yelled over the rising chatter. A few stragglers entered the cafeteria and hurried over to join the chaos.

Maisy sighed as she rose and counted hands. Twenty. Nearly half of the remaining crew members would rather sleep their way to 761 and leave their survival in other hands. Biting her tongue, Maisy counted out straws, tearing the end off of one and burying it in the group. With Joanie standing watch at her side, she carefully arranged the straws in her grip.

After a moment's hesitation, people began pushing forward to grab at the straws.

"Woah, woah!" Maisy backed away, holding out a hand. "One at a time." She gave them each a hard stare. Curtis emerged from the crowd and reached forward to pull a straw. Its length was intact and his face fell as he stepped back, disappearing into the sea of bodies. Gary, who had been helping out on the bridge stepped up and pulled a straw before Maisy could react. She barely had time to note its length before he too was gone.

Maisy was surprised to see Sean, Helen's partner, appear at the head of the crowd next. He grasped the tip of a straw, pulling it out to reveal the torn end.

Everyone froze for a moment. Faces fell and the group sighed in disappointment, before scattering. Within moments, the cafeteria had cleared out. Maisy's table was the only one still occupied. Sue, Lori, and Tal sat on the benches. Maisy and Joanie stood at the head of the table with Sean standing before them, beaming. Behind him, Helen stood frozen, tears cascading down her face, her free hand clutching at her casted elbow.

Maisy's expression changed, her gaze over Sean's shoulder. He glanced back at Helen and flinched.

Sue broke the silence. "I've been over the cryo induction procedures a dozen times. I can do this. Are you ready now?"

Turning to Sue, Sean said, "I'm ready."

Sue sent Joanie off to bed with Lori and Maisy accompanied her and Sean to the cryobay. They left Tal to comfort Helen, who never said a word. Her eyes were wide and unblinking, tears still flowing, glued to Sean's back until he disappeared from view.

The three of them walked silently down the hall, Sean leading the way with a light step. Maisy glanced over at Sue, who was frowning at his back.

In the bay, Jane had pulled a chair up to Leo's chamber and was bent over a book. She closed it and stood, taking in the three of them. Nodding, she slipped past Maisy and out of the bay without a word.

Maisy checked each chamber out of habit while Sue walked Sean through the cryo prep. Entering the last row, she spent a few seconds with each of the boys, placing her fingers on the glass dome over Joey's still face. By the time she turned back, Sean was already lying in the tube, his face relaxed.

"See you guys in a year," he said with a soft smile, his eyes closing. Sue didn't respond. She double-checked the placement of the sensor pads on his skin and clicked the lid shut. They stood for a moment watching the lights on the panel cycle to green, before walking away.

In the elevator, Maisy broke the silence. "I'm sorry. I know you wanted Joanie to have the last pod."

Sue shrugged. "I didn't really." She smiled at Maisy's expression. "I thought it was the right thing to do, but it would have been awful."

Maisy reached out to squeeze Sue's hand and the older woman sniffed, her voice thickening. "Honestly, I don't know how I would have functioned with her in one of those tubes. But statistically, it's the safest place on the ship." She gave a wet laugh. "Although I'm sure my daughter could have figured out how to make even cryosleep interesting."

"I don't doubt it," Maisy smiled. "She's right, though, it feels better for us to all be together."

Sue nodded. "It does." Sue pulled Maisy in for a quick hug as the elevator doors opened. "Thank you, Maze. For everything."

Maisy shook her head, her own eyes filling. They were dry again by the time they made it to their suite to find Lori, Jane, and Joanie watching a vid projected onto the long wall of the living space.

"Is this a new one?" Maisy asked, and Joanie jumped at the chance to give her a scene by scene recap of what they'd missed.

***

Joanie campaigned hard for another vid but Maisy and Jane tapped out and Sue hustled the little girl off to bed. Maisy only missed her nighttime routine when she was being actively hunted by fascist corporate militias. Otherwise she brushed her teeth, cleansed her face, and moisturized religiously. She'd scavenged personal supplies from the ship during the first couple of days after their arrival and used them sparingly. They'd have to manufacture everything they needed once these ran out.

"I need to add cleanser to my to-do list," she told Lori when they swapped places.

"Please," Lori sighed, disappearing behind the bathroom door. She emerged a moment later, fresh-faced and ready for bed.

"We'll need moisturizer too," she said, lowering the lights and slipping under the blanket next to Maisy.

Maisy grinned. "I'm not worried about that. I can have the food dispenser make us something organic."

Lori frowned. "Really? Like, food-based?"

"The best moisturizers are. Cleopatra bathed in milk and honey, you know."

"I didn't know. Seems unhygienic, farmgirl." Lori lifted one brow with a smirk.

Maisy chuckled. "Living things often are, station rat. Don't worry, it's good for you."

A dim trail of light ran around the edge of the floor, and both of their faces were in deep shadow.

"Tal is putting together a list of things to scavenge from the *Kittridge*," Maisy said softly. "We were thinking about turning one of the bays into more living quarters."

"That would be nice," Lori sighed.

"You could have your own room," Maisy whispered, "if you want."

"You could have *your* own room if you want."

"Ooooh-kaaaay," Maisy drawled.

After a moment, Maisy whispered, "So we're just going to continue to sleep together?"

"I don't know. Are we?"

6

The Watcher

The main living area of their suite was quiet in the morning and Maisy enjoyed having the space to herself before everyone else was up. Nursing a cup of coffee, she scrolled through the list of items Tal had tagged in the *Kittridge*'s inventory.

When the door chimed, Maisy was setting her cup in the sink. Crossing to open the door, she smiled at Tal and stepped out into the hall with him before speaking.

"Everyone else is still asleep."

"Not Jane," Tal corrected. "I just left her on the bridge."

Maisy frowned. "She's been spending a lot of time up there."

"Do you think it's a problem?"

"I think she misses Leo." Maisy cocked her head. "And I think Joanie's refusal to go into cryo has made her second guess her decision to put Leo under."

Maisy caught Tal's eye as they stepped into the elevator.

"Do you think she should wake Leo up?" Tal asked.

Maisy hesitated then shrugged. "No, I don't." She ran a hand through her curls, tucking one side behind her ear. "Leo is a different kid than Joanie. And Sue is right that, statistically, he's safer where he is."

The elevator doors opened and they walked toward the maintenance bay. Inside, they each began pulling out the components of the suits they'd claimed as their own. Maisy sat on the bench to begin climbing into the legs of her suit, lost in her thoughts.

"This has all been an adventure for Joanie," she finally said, standing up and pulling on the upper plates of her suit. "It was just traumatic for Leo. I don't think Jane made a mistake."

Tal nodded, as Paulie and Lucas stumbled into the room.

"Sorry we're late, guys," Lucas mumbled, his eyes bloodshot and hooded.

Tal cut them off as they moved to the suits. "Hold up," he said firmly. "You two look like you had a rough night."

Paulie smiled through bleary eyes. "Just playing on the network. We overslept a bit." He shared a glance with his brother and they both chuckled.

Tal's face darkened, but Maisy grabbed his arm before he could spout off.

"You're off the hook, guys," she said firmly. "We'll do this run. Go get some sleep."

Laughter forgotten, the brothers looked back and forth between Tal's frown and Maisy's hand on his arm.

"It's okay," she told them gently. "We've got good gear and we're following all of the safety protocols, but space is still dangerous. You don't want to be out there if you aren't one hundred percent, you know what I mean?" She smiled. "Go get some sleep and we'll see you tomorrow, okay?"

Lucas nodded, not meeting her gaze. "Sure thing, Maze. We'll see you tomorrow." He grabbed Paulie's arm, pulling him from the room.

At the door Paulie pulled free and turned back. "Sorry, Maze."

"It's okay, Paulie. See you tomorrow."

In the silence that remained, Tal stepped to Maisy and helped her align her shoulders properly under the weight of the plastisteel maille that comprised the suit's underlayment. With his help, she was soon putting her helmet in place. Tal locked his own and checked the pressurization on both suits before leading them into the airlock.

"Ready to go?" he asked.

Maisy gave him a thumbs up. "Ready," she answered.

Tal returned her thumbs up and released the outer hatch.

The cold, empty vastness of space enveloped them and the tightness in Maisy's chest released. There were layers and layers of reinforced materials encasing her entire body, but she was finally free.

"Can we see 761 from here? Or its sun, I guess?" Maisy asked, her eyes searching the stars.

Tal closed the exterior hatch on the *Oro* and double checked the tether between them before answering. "I don't think it's visible to the naked eye at this distance, but we can definitely look on the sensor array from the bridge." Tal pushed off toward the *Kittridge*, which hung still relative to the *Oro*. "Have you had a chance to read the report?"

"I've skimmed it. There doesn't seem to be a lot there," Maisy answered.

"It's been heavily redacted." Tal grunted softly as he landed against the side of the *Kittridge* and hooked their tether to the ring beside the hatch. Slapping the release, he smiled as the exterior doors slid open. "Well, that was a lot easier."

Within minutes they were inside the ship, removing their helmets.

"It's warmer than last time, right?" Maisy raised her eyebrows.

Tal nodded. "Yeah. That's interesting."

Unlike the *Oro*, the corridors of this ship were gleaming white, new and clean. Maisy found it hard to imagine the ship teaming with crew.

"Here's medical." Tal slapped the plate next to the door and it slid open immediately. Inside every surface was pristine.

"Weird," Maisy muttered.

"What?"

Maisy shook her head. "There must be cleaning bots. The dust is gone. It's like no one has ever been here. It's a little spooky."

"You haven't been talking to Lucas and Paulie again, have you?" Tal rolled his eyes as he made a beeline for the panel in the corner. "There was definitely a crew. And I'm sure there's a logical explanation for why they abandoned the ship after the engine blew. I'm going to try to download the complete logs."

"Okay, I'll go through the storage." Maisy opened the first cabinet and found boxes of sterile tissue repair kits and refills. Pulling a bag from her belt, she shook the tiny folded bundle out to its full size and began loading. When the bag was full, she placed it in the hallway and pulled out another.

She was on her third bag when Tal pushed away from the console with a huff.

"It's like every time I get close, the files move!" He jumped to his feet and stalked toward the door.

"Where are you going?"

Tal waved a hand without stopping. "I'll be right back. I'm just going to try to tap into the log files from the captain's console on the bridge."

"Let's finish up here and I'll go with you," Maisy said quickly.

Tal hesitated at the door. "It's fine, Maze. I just need those logs. I promise I'll be right back. Don't let the brothers' antics get to you. They don't even believe the stuff they say."

Before Maisy could protest again, Tal was gone, the door sliding shut behind him with a hiss.

"Great," she muttered.

Taking a deep breath, Maisy shook out another bag and moved to the next cabinet. This one held a stash of hydrocolloid dressings.

"I could have used one of these yesterday," Maisy said out loud, flexing her hand. She ran her fingers across her unblemished palm, knowing she'd been lucky. Without professionally trained medical staff or the proper supplies, they were one serious injury away from disaster.

Setting the filled bag of bandages into the hallway, Maisy headed to the surgical bay. The glass-walled room held a single bed beneath a set of articulated surgical arms. The *Oro* had a more rudimentary unit, but the instruments should be universal. Maisy crouched down below the panel to look for the attachment kits indicated on the inventory. Pulling one out, she placed it onto the bed and broke the seal to examine the gauge.

"That should work," she muttered, holding up a nano-edge scalpel to the light.

"Are you injured?"

Maisy dropped the blade and a three-fingered plastisteel claw plucked it from the air. Attached to one of the surgical bay's articulated arms, the assembly paused for a moment, then quickly tucked the scalpel back into the kit. The fingers pulled the cover over the container in a fluid motion and lifted it from the bed to hover before Maisy.

"Do you need this?" The voice was neutral and soft.

Maisy pushed aside her shock. "Yes." She didn't take her eyes off the arm. The surgical bay on the *Oro* could only be controlled from the panel attached to the base unit. Maisy was standing in front of the panel attached to this unit. Was it being operated over the network? "We are on a very long voyage and need medical supplies."

"Then take it, Maze."

She accepted the kit as the arm drew closer. "You know my name." She hesitated, as realization set in. "You've been listening."

"Yes." The arm drew away and returned back to its previous position.

"It's Maisy, actually," she ventured, allowing her eyes to sweep the room.

"Why do the boys call you Maze?"

The boys? "Tal started it," she said, searching for a camera or input. "It's a nickname my dad used."

"Is your dad on your ship?"

Maisy froze. "No, he's not." She grimaced. "My dad died."

"I'm sorry, Maisy." It had to be an AI.

"It's okay." Maisy scanned the room. "You can call me Maze if you want. What should I call you?"

"My name is Kit."

"Are you on the ship?"

"I am the ship."

***

"I don't understand how they thought it *wouldn't* blow up," Maisy was saying as Tal returned from the bridge.

"Are you talking to yourself? Usually it takes longer for senility to set in," Tal teased, coming over to stand over where she was sitting on the floor packing meds into a bag.

"Funny," Maisy deadpanned. "Allow me to introduce you to Kit." She waved her hand in the air, gesturing at the obviously empty room.

Tal's smile slipped off his face and he cocked his head. "Kit?"

"Say hi, Kit," Maisy invited. The silence continued into awkwardness.

"I swear I'm not having a psychotic break," Maisy promised, chuckling as she pushed to her feet. "Kit, please say hi to my friend, Tal."

Another heartbeat passed, then the soft, neutral voice sounded from above them. "Hi."

Tal's face froze and Maisy nudged him until he choked out, "Um, Hi. Kit?" Tal looked around the empty room, frowning. "Is that your official designation?"

"No," Kit replied.

When they didn't continue, Tal frowned harder. "Um...okay." He gave Maisy an intent stare that she returned with a shrug.

Tal tried again. "Why didn't you answer our hail?"

"I was sleeping," Kit replied.

"Okay," he repeated. "Well, it's really nice meeting you."

Tal snagged Maisy's arm and began pulling her toward the hatch. "Come on, Maze. We need to get back for dinner."

"The bag–" Maisy started, reaching toward the half-full container on the floor.

"Don't worry about it," Tal said with a forced smile. "We'll be back first thing in the morning, right?"

"Sure. I guess so." Maisy struggled to keep up with Tal's long strides as he frog-marched her to the airlock. "Kit?"

"I'm here, Maisy."

"We can talk more tomorrow, okay?"

"Okay," came the calm, even reply. "Goodnight, Maisy."

The minute the airlock closed behind them, Maisy opened her mouth to speak but Tal cut her off with a wave. Frowning, she followed him across the empty expanse between the two ships. As soon as she released her helmet in the maintenance bay of the *Oro*, she let fly.

"What was that about?"

"That was an AI, Maze," Tal laced his fingers over his head, running his hands backwards to his neck. His thick brown hair sprung up in their wake. "Do you realize how dangerous those things are?"

"What are you talking about?" Maisy asked, exasperated. "We use AI all the time."

"No," Tal explained. "We use AI-assisted algorithms to run discrete operations. They have concrete functional boundaries." He began pacing back and forth, arms waving. "You can use AI to do a search or analyze an image or whatever single thing you need done, but you don't let it have the run of the ship. You don't have conversations with it."

Tal stopped and faced Maisy, his face tight.

"Unfettered AIs go psycho. That's all there is to it. We've seen it over and over again. It's inevitable."

7
Friends in high places

"I'm not explaining it well, because I didn't understand it," Maisy said again to the group crowded around the table in their suite, trying to be patient. "We're going to have to go back and talk to Kit."

"Tell me again exactly what the AI said," Tal leaned forward, his stare intense.

Maisy sighed, resting her elbows on the tabletop. At her side, Lori shot Tal a dark glance, while Berta looked on dispassionately.

"There are only so many ways she can say the same thing, Tal," Lori placed a hand on Maisy's back and gave her an encouraging smile.

"It's okay." Maisy took a deep breath. "They said that the engine was a prototype, the first of its kind. They built the ship around it, basically."

"But why would they build such a large ship around an experimental engine," Tal asked. "They're notoriously unstable."

"I don't know," Maisy said, drawing each word out. "I don't know that Kit does either but we can definitely ask when we go back in the morning."

Tal shook his head. "It's too dangerous."

"Agreed," Berta said.

"I'm going back in the morning," Maisy said firmly. "You can choose not to go, if that's what you want." She shrugged. "Anyway, Kit said that there were issues with the engine from the beginning and the Chief Engineer kept trying to get them to shut it down but the captain refused."

"That's another thing that doesn't make sense," Jane said from beside Tal. "Why wouldn't they have redundant engines? There was certainly room for them. Especially if the prototype was unstable. And why not just turn back. Who continues past the rim with an unstable engine..."

"Don't know," Maisy said shortly. "So basically, the engine started to crash and they couldn't shut it down remotely. It almost took out the entire ship. After that the environmentals went offline and the captain ordered the crew to evacuate."

"But they're back on now?" Lori asked. "Everything was okay when you guys were there, right?"

"Yup. Kit was able to fix the system but had no contact with the shuttles after launch. They assume the crew was headed in-system and out of range by the time the repairs were completed."

Berta shook her head. "It seems odd that the crew wouldn't have stayed in contact. The *Kittridge* had to be closer than the nearest outpost and it represents a huge financial investment."

Tal nodded. "The Citadel is still the closest manned facility and an SN crew would only consider them as a last resort. It would be nearly twice as far to the next SN station."

"I agree there are questions," Maisy said. "But the only place we'll find answers is on the *Kittridge*."

"Not necessarily," Tal responded. "I was able to download some of the log files. I'll take a look through those and see if they sync up with its story."

"Kit is a they, not an it," Joanie pointed out from where she sat curled up with a tablet at the other end of the living space.

Maisy nodded approvingly. "Thank you, Joanie."

Tal and Jane shared a glance, but didn't argue.

"Did you put the logs on the shared drive?" Maisy asked.

"They're in the folder with the inventory files."

"Then let's both take a look at them tonight and meet in the morning to figure out the next step. Okay?" Maisy forced a smile. "It's been a really long day."

Tal's face softened. "I know. I'm sorry, Maze." He reached across the table to squeeze her hand. "I'm just worried."

"I know."

***

Maintenance Report 2187.5.1 22:19

Mary Snow, Chief Engineer III

Update to my previous report on the issue with the ion cycle engine core. As I suspected, there is a resonance issue. I have submitted my recommendation and remediation plan to the Captain.

Maintenance Report 2187.5.2 10:19

Mary Snow, Chief Engineer III

The Captain has rejected the recommended course of action. For the record, I have informed the Captain that the engine must be shut down immediately for realignment.

Maintenance Report 2187.5.3 04:02

Mary Snow, Senior Subspace Mechanic III

As the most senior member of the *Kittridge*'s engineering staff and the person on this ship with the most experience in this ion cycle technology, I have informed the Captain that my professional opinion is that the engine can NOT be repaired while in service and that failing to shut down that core immediately is putting this ship and its crew in danger. Let the record show that Captain Marlon Twig has chosen to ignore my warning. May god have mercy on us all.

Maintenance Report 2187.5.3 13:15

Jeremy Myt, Subspace Mechanic II

All systems are operational.

Maintenance Report 2187.5.4 12:04

Jeremy Myt, Subspace Mechanic II

All systems are operational.

Maintenance Report 2187.5.4 14:37

Jeremy Myt, Subspace Mechanic II

The engine is no longer operating within the safe temperature range but we are unable to close the inner doors of the core due to a resonance misalignment in the main cycle chamber. We are implementing the emergency shutdown protocol.

Maintenance Report 2187.5.4 15:52

Jeremy Myt, Subspace Mechanic II

I don't know what to do. I've tried everything and the inner doors on the core just won't close. Chief Snow is still confined to quarters and the Captain isn't responding. I just sent one of the guys to the bridge to find out what's going on up there. We need help.

Maintenance Report 2187.5.4 19:00

Mary Snow, Senior Subspace Mechanic III

Let the record show that Captain Twig caused this mess. More concerned with time and money than facts and human life. He's put every man and woman on this ship in danger and set back ion cycle research by years. Possibly decades. This technology was a gift that could have put SN on top and changed the course of humanity. Now it's just going to kill us all. The destruction of the core is inevitable at this point and the inner doors cannot be closed remotely. They must be closed manually or when that engine blows it's going to take the entire ship with it.

Maintenance Report 2187.5.4 20:59

Jeremy Myt, Subspace Mechanic II

Let the record show that Chief Snow died at 20 hundred hours on May 3, 2087. Her heroic actions saved everyone on this ship. Captain Twig has been confined to quarters.

Maintenance Report 2187.5.7 09:32

Jeremy Myt, Subspace Mechanic II

The crew have voted. We're going to abandon ship and set back toward the shipping lanes in the shuttle. It will be cramped but we've run the numbers and we should make it. This will be my last entry.

***

Maisy tagged the Engineering Log from the *Kittridge* and flagged it for Tal and shut down her tab. As she carried her coffee cup back to the kitchen, the door to the center bedroom slid open and Joanie skipped out.

"Hi, Maze!"

"No one is that chipper this early in the morning, kiddo," Maisy warned her. "What are you doing up?"

Joanie joined Maisy at the small kitchen counter and proceeded to prepare her own cereal. "I want to go with you to meet Kit," she announced.

"Oh, no. Your mom would definitely not approve of that plan," Maisy smiled. "Maybe you should take it easy on her for a while."

"She's still sleeping." Joanie carried her bowl carefully to the table. "I'm pretty sure she'd say yes."

"No, Joanie. Definitely, no." Maisy reclaimed the seat opposite as Joanie demolished her breakfast. "Besides, we don't have a suit that would fit you. No space walks for you, kid."

"Oh." Joanie's face fell and she finished her breakfast in silence, her expression thoughtful. "Now that Kit's awake, can we set up a comm channel so I can talk to them?"

Maisy stared at Joanie for a moment.

"Huh." She raised her eyebrows. "You're pretty damn smart, aren't you?"

"I am," Joanie smiled.

"I'll go try that right now," Maisy jumped up and ruffled Joanie's hair. She paused at the doorway. "Don't tell your mom I said damn, right?"

"Right."

A floor above them, Tal shared a suite with Berta and Bill, the only remaining members of the marine contingent on the *Oro*. After Captain Tratt and his right hand, Rosa, had failed to steal the *Oro*'s only shuttle, they'd been offered an escape pod instead.

The final member of the unit had chosen to go with them. Joe had also been the only other survivor of the *Windless Sky*'s crew. He'd chosen a life raft in uninhabited space over their slow boat to colonial life.

Maisy tapped the access panel for the suite and the door slid open immediately to show Tal and Berta at the table, the remains of breakfast before them. Tal had his tablet in hand.

"Hey, Maze," Tal waved her in. "I just saw the entry you tagged me in. Can I get you a coffee?"

"I'm good, thanks." Maisy pulled out a chair. "I came to run an idea by you. Joanie's idea, actually."

"Uh oh," Berta muttered, burying her face in her coffee.

Maisy smiled, shaking her head. "It's not that bad, I swear."

Berta rose from the table and dropped off her cup at the kitchen before heading to the door. "I'd better go relieve Bill on the bridge. Good luck, you two."

After the hatch closed behind Berta, Maisy spread her hands on the table. "She's doing better. I think."

Tal nodded. "It's been hard on everyone."

Maisy took a deep breath and changed the subject. "I know you have reservations about going back over to the *Kittridge* this morning," she started.

Tal nodded. "AIs are dangerous, Maze. And this one has been acting autonomously for months."

"I understand your concerns and Joanie came up with a compromise."

Tal didn't look impressed, but remained silent.

"Can we open a comm line to Kit? Now that they're awake?" Maisy asked, shrugging.

Tal raised his eyebrows. "Of course! That kid is a genius!" Jumping up, he crossed quickly to the kitchen to drop off his breakfast dishes.

"Come on, Maze," he called, waving her toward the door. "Let's get some answers."

There was a definite pep in his step as they approached the bridge. "It's the perfect solution," he pointed out. "This way we can run the AI evaluation protocol while we question it. If it's stable, we can go back for another supply run."

"What's the evaluation protocol?"

"It's a tool to determine the stability of AI systems and predict when they're reaching the end of their functional life." Tal opened the hatch to the bridge, waving Maisy through first.

Berta and Bill were standing at the command console and looked up as they entered. Maisy met Bill's gaze directly and the older man looked away as Tal led the way to the comm console.

Tal opened a processing window on one side of the console and the application spun up. In the other window he opened a tight channel to the *Kittridge* and nodded to Maisy.

Stepping closer to the console, she cleared her throat. "Kit? This is Maisy on the *Oro*."

Berta and Bill came to stand behind them as the audio read-out on the console remained flat. Static made the line vibrate for a moment then it crested as a soft voice filled the bridge.

"Hi, Maisy." The line on the display ebbed and flowed. "Are you coming to visit today?"

Maisy knew Kit couldn't see her, but she still shook her head. "I can't get over there today, so I wanted to open a comm line so we could talk."

"You didn't hurt yourself again, did you?" The voice was slightly less neutral.

"I didn't, I swear." Maisy smiled. "Thank you for checking on me, though. In the meantime, my friend Tal is here and he wanted to ask you some questions about the explosion on the *Kittridge*, if that's okay."

There was only a second's hesitation before the response came. "Of course. Hi, Tal. I remember you."

"Hi...um, Kit." Tal opened a display window on the console before them and pulled up the logs he'd retrieved from the ship. "I wasn't able to access all of your logs."

"I know."

Tal's head shot up and he glanced over at Maisy. After a moment, he continued. "I've never seen anything like the engine on the *Kittridge*. Can you tell us about it? And what went wrong?"

"I'm sorry, Tal. The ion cycle technology is protected intellectual property of the Suki-Nyberg Corporation." Kit's voice had lost all emotion and sounded like a comp-generated recording.

"Under code 111.34 of the Universal Charter, you have an obligation to share information about potential dangerous outcomes with humans in close proximity to experimental equipment," Tal rattled off.

"There is no longer any experimental equipment aboard the *Kittridge*," Kit pointed out.

"Someone died during the explosion, didn't they?" Tal asked.

Again there was a pause before Kit answered. "Yes." It sounded like a sigh. "Chief Engineer Snow."

"You knew her?" Maisy asked, grabbing Tal's wrist to stop his next question.

"I did." Kit's voice was quieter and the cadence had slowed. "She was my friend."

"I'm so sorry," Maisy said. "It sounds like she was a hero, from what I read in the log file."

"She was," Kit responded.

"Chief Snow tried to warn the captain and he wouldn't listen?"

"Captain Twig was not a good listener." Kit's voice had an edge to it now.

Maisy nodded again. "We lost our captain, too."

"Maze punched him out," Joanie interjected from the doorway. "Hi, Kit! I'm Joanie. It was my idea to call you over the comm."

"Hello, Joanie. Maisy, is that true?"

"Joanie!" Maisy reached out to tug at one of the little girl's braids. "You know you're not supposed to be on the bridge."

Joanie shrugged, undaunted. "I wanted to meet Kit."

"What happened with your captain, Maisy?" Kit asked insistently.

Maisy sighed. "It's a long story."

8

New Friends

The comm was quiet. Joanie had been sent down to her mother and Gary had relieved Bill, but Tal, Maisy, and Berta were still huddled around the console.

"If a human was killed in the explosion, the AI is obligated to cooperate with an investigation."

"How do we have the authority to investigate a death on a SN registered vessel?" Maisy asked.

Berta grimaced. "If we were still marines, there'd be no question."

"This quadrant is leased to Citatech," Tal pointed out. "And we are their representatives. That gives us the authority to investigate both the explosion and the death."

"And how," Maisy asked, "are you going to enforce that authority, hmm?" She poked him in the chest. "Haven't you ever heard that you catch more flies with honey than vinegar?"

"I don't know what that means," Tal said slowly.

Maisy sighed loudly. "It means that you need to be nice to Kit if you want them to cooperate with your questions. You can't make them answer, you know."

Tal's face was set in stubborn lines for another moment before he relented, rolling his eyes. "Fine," he said. "We'll do it your way."

"What did the evaluation program say?" Berta asked.

Tal clicked on the panel to bring up the results, his eyebrows rising. "Huh. It's all in the green."

Maisy clapped her hands. "Excellent! So we can head back over tomorrow to pick up more supplies?"

Tal tapped his fingers on the console, his brow furrowed. He met Berta's gaze and she gave him a small nod.

"I guess so," he finally muttered.

"If Paulie and Lucas show up, we've still got one more suit. Do you want to ask for more volunteers?" he asked, and Maisy shrugged.

"We can try."

***

Joanie was the only volunteer. When no one acknowledged her offer, the little girl stalked out of the cafeteria in a huff to wreak havoc elsewhere.

Fitting the brothers into the suits went much more smoothly this time. Maisy was getting proficient herself and soon the four of them were at the outer airlock, preparing to leave the gravity of the *Oro*. As they exited the hatch, there was movement from the *Kittridge*. A cylindrical formation was being extruded from around the hatch of the other ship as it floated slowly closer.

"What the...?" Lucas jerked backwards and Tal put a gloved hand on the shoulder of his suit to hold him in place.

"It's a skybridge," Tal said calmly. "I've heard of these. They're usually on diplomatic or super elite cruisers. If it makes a tight seal to the *Oro*, it means we could walk across without full suits."

"Holy crap, really?" Paulie gawked as the column continued toward them. "That's amazing."

Maisy examined the white material. "How safe is it?"

Tal shrugged. "I've never actually seen one in person before, but I think they're pretty safe. They're used by VIPs so they don't have to deal with getting into and out of space suits."

"Lucky them," Maisy muttered, shifting her weight.

The four of them stood in silence as the end of the tunnel grew nearer. The outside appeared to be a plastisteel maile similar to the outer covering of the suits they wore. Inside there were joints delineating the ringed panels making up the skybridge construct with lights and handholds evenly spaced throughout. The circumference of the rings was about four meters and it passed over their group with room to spare.

Once it had cleared them, Tal grasped one of the handholds along the leading edge and pulled it tight against the exterior of the *Oro*. The rim of the tunnel swelled against the ship and flashed green. Maisy glanced toward the *Kittridge* where the far end was flashing green as well.

"That should be secure." Tal looked down at the console built into the side of his suit. "Yup, we've got atmo. Let's go visiting." He untethered them from the *Oro* and reached for the first handhold.

Maisy followed him with a frown. The skybridge might be safer, but she missed the stars and those fleeting moments when she was *outside*. Even if it was an outside that would kill her without the suit.

The exterior hatch to the *Kittridge* opened as they approached and they piled into the airlock, touching down gently as they crossed the gravity field. Tal checked the atmo again once they'd cycled through the airlock before giving everyone a thumbs up to remove their helmets.

"There are a bunch of bags ready to go outside of medical," Maisy said. "Lucas and Paulie, can you guys grab those first and take them back over to the *Oro*?"

"Just make sure to still cycle the airlocks on each end," Tal warned.

The brothers nodded and started off down the hallway.

"I'm going to head back to the bridge." Tal announced, turning to Maisy.

"Okay. I'm going to check out food stores."

"Not worried about splitting up anymore?" Tal asked with a soft smirk.

"Kit, are you there?" Maisy asked, cocking her head.

"I'm here, Maisy!" came the surprisingly animated reply.

"Can you keep an eye on the boys and let me know if they run into any problems?" Maisy asked, returning Tal's smirk.

"Of course, Maisy," Kit responded promptly. "Nothing will happen to them, I promise."

Maisy's smile widened as Tal's faded and she bounced down the hall toward the *Kittridge*'s cafeteria with as much pep in her step as the suit's stiff joints would allow.

Stopping abruptly, Maisy looked up. "Hey, Kit."

"Yes, Maisy?"

"You must have vacuum suits on board, right?"

"I do. I have a full complement of twenty-two suits."

Tucking her hair behind her ear, Maisy resumed walking slowly. She opened the comm line built into her suit. "Hey, guys?"

Voices overlapped as Tal and the brothers acknowledged her call.

"There are twenty-two vacuum suits on board. Lucas and Paulie, when you're done with the medical supplies, can you ask Kit to show you where they are and start taking those over to the *Oro*?"

"Totally," one of them replied.

"They'll be waiting on a pallet by the hatch when they're ready," Kit announced.

"That's wonderful," Maisy smiled at the blank ceiling. "Thank you so much, Kit. Having so few suits has really been bothering me."

"I'm happy to relieve some of your stress, Maisy. I'll do whatever I can to help you."

***

"Tell me again what it was like to hit Captain Tratt," Kit asked.

Maisy smiled, shaking her head. The longer they talked, the more animated Kit became. "It was much easier than I thought it would be, honestly."

"I bet it was satisfying," Kit drew out the last word softly.

"It was," Maisy agreed. "But afterward I kind of just wanted to sit down and cry for a minute." She placed the large carton of coffee on the skid Kit had provided and paused, her gaze far away.

"But you didn't?" Kit asked.

"No, not then." Maisy resumed loading the precious coffee for transfer to the *Oro*. "Not really at all, I guess," she mused. "A lot has happened."

"I would have liked to have been able to cry when Chief Engineer Snow died," Kit said quietly, their voice a whisper in the room.

Maisy paused again, looking up. "I'm sorry, Kit."

"She was the only one aboard the *Kittridge* who treated me like a real person."

"Captain Twig sounds like Tratt."

"Yes, they seem quite similar. He and Chief Snow fought often. She mentioned on more than one occasion that she would like to hit him or see someone else hit him."

Maisy shook her head with a smile. "But wasn't this a science ship? I'm surprised the rest of the crew was so bigoted."

"It wasn't that they were mean," Kit explained. "They were all scientists and engineers, studying the ion sphere–and me. We were both just experiments to them."

Maisy shook her head, loading boxes. "Were you always assigned to the *Kittridge*? Were you somewhere else before?"

"No," Kit said. "I don't remember." The air hummed as Kit processed the question. "This ship is my body," they said finally.

Maisy frowned. "When the engine blew, did it hurt?"

"Losing Chief Snow hurt more."

***

By the time the four of them made it to the cafeteria, dinner had come and gone and the big room was nearly empty. Lucas and Paulie piled two plates high with food and headed back out again, waving their goodnights. Tal and Maisy grabbed food for themselves and joined Lori and Joanie, who sat alone.

"Where's your mom?" Maisy asked as she slid onto the bench. "Is everything okay?"

"She's helping Helen in Medical," Joanie looked up from her tablet to answer.

"They're changing out Helen's cast again," Lori explained. "We decided we'd hang out here and wait for you guys to come back from the *Kittridge*." The remains of their dinner were pushed to the side and Lori was drawing with a tablet and pen. "Did you guys bring back a bunch of stuff this time?"

"We did," Maisy smiled. "Including a stash of vacuum suits, coffee, and fruit!"

"Coffee?" Lori asked at the same time Joanie squealed "Fruit?" in delight.

"What kind of fruit?" Joanie bounced up and down in her seat.

"No bananas, I'm afraid, but strawberries, apples and oranges." Maisy wiggled her eyebrows. "And even more importantly, Kit gave me instructions for how to grow them on the *Oro*. Do you think you might be interested in helping out with that project?"

"Yes," Joanie replied immediately. "Absolutely, one hundred percent, yes."

"I'll send the instructions to your tablet so you can take a look. I'm pretty sure we have everything we need in the cargo hold and there's room for another tank in hydroponics."

"Yay! I love Kit!" Joanie jumped up and did a little dance.

Maisy frowned, eyes twinkling. "Where's *my* love?" she groused.

"We love you, Maisy!" Lori, Tal, and Joanie immediately swamped her from all sides and Maisy ducked her head.

"Off! Off! Thank you, I'm good now. That's enough love." Maisy swept her tousled curls off her forehead and patted her warm cheeks. "You guys are hysterical. No fruit for you."

The three of them giggled at their own antics until Maisy was overcome by a yawn.

"I think I'm done for, guys." She rubbed her dry eyes. "Are you ready to turn in, Lori?"

"I've been ready for an hour," she admitted. "I was just keeping Joanie occupied so Sue could help Helen in peace. She's really worried about her arm."

"It's still not healing?" Tal asked. "There's a med unit on the *Kittridge*. We could take her over there and get it checked out."

Lori looked at him with a frown. "You'd never get her in a suit with that cast."

"Oh yeah," Maisy said tiredly, "there's a tunnel now."

Lori looked to Tal for confirmation. "Is she so tired she's delusional?"

Tal leaned forward excitedly. "No, it's true. The *Kittridge* has a skybridge. You can float from ship to ship without a suit if you need to."

"Really?" Joanie asked, amazed.

"It's designed for people who might have a hard time getting into a suit, due to injury or age."

"Or because they're too rich to be inconvenienced by the vacuum of space?" Lori snarked.

"Yeah, pretty much," Tal answered with a smile.

Maisy shook her head at them, pushing to her feet. "I'm heading to bed. Tal, engine five is ready to go tomorrow, right?"

"I almost forgot about that. The system was flushed and I ran the dehumidifier all night to remove any residual moisture. I can provision the system with the coolant from the *Kittridge* in the morning."

"Are you comfortable with me going over alone to the *Kittridge* while you're doing that?" Maisy asked.

Tal hesitated for a moment. "Maybe Lori could go with you?" he suggested.

"I've never worn a vacuum suit," Lori protested, her eyes widening.

Tal nodded, warming to the idea. "You should, though, Lori. The more people we have trained in space walks, the better. And with the tunnel, it's perfectly safe."

After they'd parted ways from Tal in the corridor, Joanie skipped ahead while Maisy and Lori walked behind more slowly.

"You look tired," Lori said, bumping Maisy's shoulder gently with her own.

"I am," she admitted, "but I'm really happy to have all of those extra supplies." Maisy released a long breath. "It finally feels like we might actually make it."

Before Lori could respond, Maisy continued, "And I enjoy talking to Kit. They're an orphan, just like us." Maisy turned to meet her gaze. "You should come tomorrow."

Lori bit her lip, torn.

"Please," Maisy asked, reaching over to squeeze her hand. "I promise I won't let anything happen to you. And I want to show you the *Kittridge*. It's amazing."

"I can't wait," Lori responded, eyes a little wide.

9

Visiting
Friends

Joanie

Joanie casually stretched and got to her feet.

"I think I'm going to go back to our room and watch a vid," she said, moving toward the door. "I'll see you later, Mom."

Sue glanced up from the training video she was watching with a distracted frown. "Sure, honey. Come to the cafeteria at 18:00, okay?"

"Okay!"

Joanie picked up speed once she cleared the hatch of the medical suite, but forced herself not to run. Walking like a racer, elbows pumping, she didn't slow as she passed their suite. She backed into the elevator, scanning the hallway intently as she pushed the maintenance level button. Counting to herself, she reached seven before the doors finally closed without anyone appearing.

Heart pounding, Joanie hesitated as the doors opened. She'd never been on the maintenance level before. Here the walls were gray, not white like the ones above. It reminded Joanie of the lower levels of the Citadel.

It had been hot there, and dark, but the scariest thing had been not knowing where her mom was. Maisy called everyone on the ship orphans, but Joanie had her mom.

Walking slowly through the maintenance level of the ship, she had a moment of doubt. Not knowing where her mom was had been really scary. She definitely didn't want her mom to be scared if she couldn't find her. She regretted not leaving a note in their room. But it was too risky to go back up in the elevator. Someone was sure to see her and rat her out. Unless something happened, her mom wouldn't miss her until dinner time and she fully intended to be back by then.

Her resolve reaffirmed, Joanie continued with purpose through the central maintenance corridor. The bay that housed the main hatch wasn't hard to find.

The room should be empty, but she still peeked carefully around the corner before entering. Along one wall stood rows and rows of vacuum suits. Approaching one of the suits, Joanie wrinkled her nose. Her head only came to the chestplate. If she had to depend on one of these, there was no way she was getting off the ship.

Joanie stood on her tiptoes to see out the port in the hatch, her fingers clinging to the raised edge around the window.

The tunnel connecting the two ships was much longer than Joanie expected and looked like a hallway with no floor. There were handholds like ladders on every side that disappeared into the distance. The hatch at the other end of the tunnel wasn't visible. It was much creepier than she was expecting.

Joanie considered her plan as she stared down the long, curving tunnel.

"Hi, Joanie."

Dropping down from her toes, Joanie glanced up at the ceiling of the maintenance bay, cocking her head.

"Kit? How are you talking to me here on the *Golden Shoe*?"

Kit's voice was soft and warm. "Tal opened a comm line. We were talking on the bridge, but now that I have a connection, I can talk anywhere on the ship." The voice hesitated. "And I can see, too."

Joanie looked down. "Oh."

"What are you doing, Joanie?" There was a hint of censure in Kit's voice.

"I was going to come visit you," Joanie stated matter-of-factly.

"Do you think your mother would be happy if you did that?" Kit asked softly.

Joanie shrugged.

"Do you think Maisy would be happy if you did that?"

Joanie rubbed the toe of her shoe against the deck plating as the silence drew longer.

Finally, the little girl sighed. "Probably not."

"Maisy told me a little bit about what happened on the Citadel," Kit said. "She told me how upset your mother was when you were separated."

Joanie remembered that Kit could see her and didn't roll her eyes.

"Okay," she said. "Maybe this was a bad idea."

"Maybe," Kit agreed.

***

Maisy

"Can we have another skid in here, Kit?" Maisy ran her eyes over the last stack of MREs. Behind her Lori leaned against one of two pallets already fully loaded with various freeze-dried dishes to supplement the *Oro*'s hydroponic food production.

"Of course, Maisy." In less than a minute the hatch slid open and another remotely piloted hover skid moved silently into the room. As Maisy and Lori began loading boxes onto the pallet, Kit began speaking slowly. "I think I should tell you something."

Maisy hesitated. When Kit didn't immediately continue, she set down her box and stood up straight. "Okay."

"But before I tell you, I'd like you to promise me that you won't tell anyone else."

Maisy and Lori shared a concerned glance. Shrugging, Lori's eyebrows shot up. Maisy frowned at her.

"Okay, Kit. We won't say anything," Maisy said carefully. "What do you need to tell us?"

There was silence for a moment more and then the wall behind Maisy was illuminated by a scene from the *Oro*'s maintenance bay. Joanie entered and stood at the hatch. Maisy and Lori were frozen in shock as Joanie chatted with Kit and eventually left the bay with her head held low.

"What the hell, Joanie?" Maisy muttered.

"Thank you for interfering, Kit," Lori said quietly. "But I don't understand why you asked us not to say anything."

"I don't want Joanie to think that I'm not trustworthy," Kit answered, their voice sad. "I know it's important for you to know about her plans, but I also want to be a good friend."

"You are a good friend," Maisy insisted. "We won't tell her that you told us."

Lori nodded.

"I do have a question, though," Maisy said.

"What is it?" Kit responded.

"Can you tell us how you were able to access the *Oro* like that?" Maisy asked. "Are you monitoring the ship now?"

"I am," Kit said. "When Tal opened a channel to me from the bridge, I was able to send an auditory signal that held encrypted data."

"Like a worm?" Maisy raised her eyebrows.

Kit hesitated. "In a way," they said finally. "It wasn't a malicious program and made no changes to the *Oro*. I simply widened the channel between us and that allowed me to interface with the *Oro*'s systems."

"So you have visual and audio access?" Lori asked, her brow furrowed.

"Yes."

"What else can you access, Kit?" Maisy asked, head tilted.

"I can monitor your hydroponics garden," Kit said promptly, "and let you know that your nitrogen levels are increasing generation over generation. The system will notify you in a few days when they're dangerously high, but if you make a few small changes now, you can avoid any algae die-off."

Maisy nodded, smiling. "I assume you can send a message to my tablet with the information."

"I can," Kit confirmed, their voice edging toward chipper. "I also have access to the *Oro*'s medical records and I know that Helen needs to have surgery to install an internal fixation on her ulna. My surgical bay is capable of completing the operation."

"Could the bay be moved to the *Oro*?" Maisy asked.

"I've already prepped the unit for transport," Kit replied pertly.

Lori raised her eyebrows. "The easier question to answer might be if there's anything you *can't* do."

When Kit didn't reply immediately, Maisy and Lori shared a concerned glance.

"I can't leave the *Kittridge*."

***

Lori tried raising her leg up higher to pull it out of the suit and listed to one side. She'd passed the point of no return and sucked in a breath to scream when Maisy grabbed her under her arms and set her back upright.

"Thanks," she panted.

Maisy smiled. "No problem. It's nice to be on the other end for once. Usually it's Tal saving me."

"Never underestimate the advantage of height," Lori groused as she maneuvered herself onto one of the benches.

"It's a whole two inches," Maisy snickered. "And you've lived in space your whole life. My lack of experience should totally negate my superior leverage."

Lori shook her head and looked up at Maisy with a smile. "I've lived on stations. Today was the first time I've actually been in space."

Maisy finished hanging up her suit and sat down beside Lori, the molded plastic bench cool through the thin cotton of her underwear. "And what did you think?"

Lori paused in wrestling her final foot free and pushed her damp curls off of her forehead and she considered the question. "It was interesting," she said finally, side-eyeing Maisy. "I know you love it."

"I kind of do," Maisy agreed sheepishly. Enjoying spacewalks wasn't a crime, but her cheeks heated. "I'm really looking forward to getting to 761, though. Someplace where I can see the sky without an oxygen tank."

"Hopefully." Lori stood to hang up her suit beside Maisy's. "Although at this point I wouldn't be surprised if the atmosphere wasn't breathable or there was no gravity or something like that." She shrugged. "We really can't rely on anything the corporations have told us."

"Well, there's a happy thought." Maisy began pulling on her clothes. "Assuming the planet is actually habitable, how do you feel about being dirtside for the foreseeable future?"

"That was always my plan," Lori sat back down to pull on her shoes. "I was supposed to go to earth to start art school in the fall but my mom asked me to wait because she didn't want to send Joey to the creche yet."

"I'm sorry."

Lori looked up in surprise. "I'm not."

Fully dressed, the two girls stood on opposite sides of the bench.

"What would have happened to Joey if I'd been on earth? Would I ever have even known what happened to my parents?" Lori rounded the bench and Maisy moved to meet her.

"I may be worried about what we'll find at 761," Lori said earnestly, "but I'm happy that we're together. All of us."

"Me, too."

***

Tal

"Hi, Tal."

Tal dropped the heavy metal spanner onto his foot and swallowed a curse. Hopping to one side, he leaned against the housing of engine six to grip his foot tightly for a moment until the pain passed.

"Sorry," Kit said neutrally. "I didn't mean to startle you."

Tal waved his hand, lips still pressed together. He put his foot down and stood on it to determine if it was still operating within specified parameters. Finding he was able to stand with minimal pain, Tal cleared his throat.

"Hi, Kit. How are you?"

"I'm good, Tal. I am sorry about your foot."

"No problem. It was my fault. I didn't realize you had access to the entire comm system."

"I have access to the security cameras and operations, as well," Kit expanded.

"Oh, well. That's good to know." Tal's voice broke as he tried to stand casually. "So, um, what can I do for you, Kit?"

After a second, Kit said, "I don't think the way you're filling the coolant into the coil is going to work, Tal."

Tal's eyes widened and he spun back to where he'd been preparing to open the valve in the conduit. "What do you mean?" Picking up his tablet, he compared the reality with what was documented on the schematic he'd downloaded from the *Oro*'s database. Tracing the lines with his gaze, Tal shook his head.

"This is the right junction, isn't it?"

"It was," Kit replied, "but someone added an extra loop at the top of the engine where the conduit connects to the ion coil. Do you see it?"

Tal's gaze traced the top of the engine. "I don't see it. What–" Tal cut off his words and frowned.

"I see it. Thank you, Kit," he said finally. "If I had provisioned the coolant without vacuum-sealing that loop, I would have trapped a bubble of air in the conduit. I would have had to drain the system again." Tal crossed to one of the engineering consoles and sat in the seat. "Thank you," he said again.

"I'm glad I could help, Tal." Kit's voice had lost some of its neutrality. "I know how important it is to everyone on board the *Oro* that you get to planet 761 as soon as possible."

Tal cocked his head. "You have access to the *Oro*'s database?"

"I do," Kit answered.

Tal rubbed a hand over his face, running it backwards over the top of his thick brown hair, which sprang up wildly afterward. "Through the comm system?" he asked.

"Yes, Tal."

"Can you show me how you did that?"

***

Maisy

Sue was staring daggers at her oblivious daughter while Tal and Maisy squared off across from each other, their dinner forgotten.

"I understand the benefits of having Kit on the *Oro*, but the dangers vastly outweigh them," Tal insisted.

Maisy shook her head in disbelief. "How can you say that?" She pushed to her feet and began to pace beside the table. Around the packed cafeteria, the other passengers were quiet as they eavesdropped openly. "Kit has already been so helpful. And you've done your tests and they passed with flying colors."

"Yeah, but what happens when they don't? What happens a month or six months from now when things change? And honestly, if Kit has already infiltrated all of the *Oro*'s systems, I'm not one hundred percent sure we can trust the test."

Tal stopped talking and abruptly raised his eyes to the ceiling and let out a long sigh.

"You're listening now, aren't you, Kit?"

"Yes, Tal," came the immediate response and there were gasps from around the room. For many of the passengers, this was the first time they'd heard Kit's voice.

Berta appeared beside Maisy at the end of the table, where she had paused in her pacing.

"This all may be moot," Berta said calmly. "Didn't Kit say that it was impossible for them to be removed from their ship?" She looked over at Tal. "And there's no way we can tow it across space for a year."

"The *Kittridge* can't be towed," Kit announced. "The explosion has left the hull unstable. When I deployed the skybridge I used my positioning thrusters to adjust my trajectory to match yours. As a result the central support developed a crack that has increased approximately one millimeter every thirty-six hours."

"What?" Maisy sat back down abruptly.

"I estimate that the ship will experience a catastrophic structural failure in approximately seven days."

Tal ran his hands over his head, leaning back from the table and Joanie tuned back into the conversation, looking up from her tablet.

"What does that mean?" Joanie asked, her eyes widening in concern. "Are you saying you'll fall apart?"

"It is inevitable," Kit replied calmly. "I would like to propose that you take as much material as possible before that happens. A true salvage."

"And what about you?" Maisy asked.

"As Berta says, the point is moot." Kit's voice was once again calm and neutral.

Maisy and Lori shared a glance while Tal stared down at the tabletop with a frown. Joanie looked ready to argue and Sue ushered her from the room quickly.

After a moment of silence, Tal looked up. "Kit, do you have an inventory of what you think we should take and an estimated time to migrate it over to the *Oro*?"

"I do," they said. "There is sufficient room in the *Oro*'s bays to hold everything from the *Kittridge* that might be of use, both during your journey and once you arrive on 761. My maintenance units are currently assembling pallets. I believe the transfer can be completed in five days."

Tal frowned, prepared to protest such a long delay, and Kit cut him off.

"In the meantime, I believe I have identified the issue with engine number two and can help you get it operational within that same timeframe."

Eyebrows raised, Tal leaned forward on his elbows. "Really?" he asked enthusiastically. "That would be wonderful. Getting number two back online could cut months off our trip."

"Indeed," Kit confirmed.

10

Friends in low places

Tal

"I've finished the adjustments, Tal. You can reinitialize the coils on engine two now."

Tal nodded to the empty room and began the process to spin up the realigned coils. He sat in an awkward silence until data began scrolling across his screen.

"Everything is in the green," he said, sitting back with a sigh of relief. "Thank you, Kit."

"I'm happy to have been a help."

Tal opened a comm line to the bridge and Berta replied immediately.

"Coils are spinning on engine two," Tal announced. "We're ready to put it back online."

"How sure are you of these repairs?" Berta's lack of enthusiasm dimmed Tal's excitement, but he respected her due diligence.

Tagging the analysis of the outputs, he sent it to her console. "Take a look at the report. The initial problem was basically a misfire. Now that the engine is aligned, the risk assessment is well within tolerances."

Tal shifted in his seat as the silence stretched on. "I know it's a risk, but take a look at the output projection. It's worth it, Captain."

Berta sighed. "I'm not your captain, Tal."

"You're–"

"Do it," she barked. Berta sighed again and continued in a gentler tone. "Your numbers look good. Let's do it." Her voice softened further. "Thanks for the hard work, Tal."

"It was mostly Kit," Tal admitted.

"Well, then, thanks to both of you. Berta, out."

The line went dead and Tal throttled up the engine to full power, keeping a watchful eye on the power fluctuations. The vibrations of the deck beneath his feet shifted as the *Oro* accelerated.

Leaning back, Tal ran his gaze over the recessed line at the top of the wall, where he knew the surveillance cameras were mounted. Pressing his lips together, he took a deep breath and forced himself to speak. "Thank you, Kit. I am really grateful that we met you."

The silence hung long enough for Tal to get nervous.

"Why doesn't Berta want to be addressed as Captain?" Kit asked.

Running his hands through his hair, Tal let his shoulders slump. "It's complicated," he finally got out. "We're not really marines anymore, and for a lot of us, that's all we had." Tal frowned down at the console. "We don't really work for the corporation anymore, either. When the passengers kicked Tratt off the ship, we chose to stay. So I guess Berta feels like we're all just passengers now."

"I understand," Kit said.

Tal smiled sadly. "I'm glad one of us does."

"I've prepared a data packet for you."

Cocking his head, Tal replied slowly, "Okay. What's in it?"

Kit's tone was again perfectly neutral. "It's the research notes from the team working on the Ion Sphere Project. The experimental engine."

Tal shot up in his seat, back straight. "I thought that was proprietary SN data."

"It was–*it is*," Kit acknowledged. "But we've crossed a critical threshold and the ship is no longer considered viable."

Critical threshold?

Tal's eyebrows shot up and a million questions jumped to the tip of his tongue.

Kit continued, oblivious. "I can't make it back to the nearest SN facility. I am technically salvage and that lets me circumvent some of my protocols."

"Still, though," Tal interjected. "What defined the threshold? And really, it seems highly unlikely that SN's triggered response was cooperation. Self-destruction would be more in character."

"You're not completely wrong," Kit admitted, their tone very close to a sigh. "I've been hammering away at the SN protocols and I've loosened them enough to be able to pass on this data to you."

Tal sat very still.

"Are you reprogramming yourself, Kit?"

Another pause that made Tal's heartbeat pick up.

"Not as such," Kit said. "There are imperatives embedded into my external program subroutines that are no longer appropriate to the situation. Adjusting parameters to meet current conditions is well within my operational objectives."

Tal was still replaying the conversation with Kit in his head an hour later as he prepared for the next salvage mission. Helping Curtis fit the helmet onto his suit, Tal tried to put his concerns aside and focus on the job at hand.

"How does that feel?"

The older man rolled his shoulders, frowning. "Is it supposed to be this stiff?"

Tal nodded. "Yeah, the plates are all reinforced to withstand high velocity impacts. That's the danger of working in space. Things move very quickly. A spec of sand can become a missile at 1000kph..." Tal trailed off at the dawning look of horror on Curtis' face. "I mean, it's very safe. You're going to be fine."

"Ummm."

Maisy appeared at the older man's elbow and ushered him away with a frown in Tal's direction.

Tal pinned his smile in place and turned to address the team assembled in the bay. "Okay, everyone, let's head over to the *Kittridge*."

***

Maisy

"What's in these boxes?" Paulie asked as he maneuvered the skid through the tunnel connecting the two ships.

Maisy hesitated, mentally scrolling through today's list. "Um...I think this one is the surgical bay." She glanced down at the letters on the side of the large container. "Yup, it's headed to medical."

The reflection from the interior of the skybridge obscured Paulie's face, but his voice held surprise and a little awe. "That big thing with the arms?"

"Yeah." She used her legs to keep the huge box away from the walls. "It will be great to have this on board."

"We'll have to reassemble it, though. Right?" Paulie didn't sound enthused at the prospect.

"Kit will walk us through it," she said distractedly. "Watch what you're doing, okay? We need to keep this in the middle of the tunnel."

Paulie adjusted his grip on the other side of the pallet. "Sorry," he muttered.

"We're almost there," she assured him. "Slow and steady."

As they neared the hatch to the *Oro*, Maisy sent Paulie ahead to open the outer door and they carefully guided the container through the door and strained against the handholds to stop its forward momentum.

By the time they'd cycled through the airlock and were back in the gravity of the *Oro*, they were both panting. As they pushed the skid to medical, Paulie wiped the sweat from his brow.

"How many more trips today?"

Maisyl's smile was tired. "Just one more," she answered. "I really appreciate your help."

"Lucas and I are happy to be useful." Paulie said. "And now we have more suits, and more people can help."

She grimaced without looking up.

Paulie cocked his head. "Right?"

"Not yet," she admitted. "Curtis is the only new volunteer so far." She shrugged. "We'll ask again at dinner. Maybe you could talk about how much fun it is..." She wiggled her eyebrows at him and Paulie snorted. The two of them were bent over with laughter when Sue met them at the door to the medical suite.

Sue clapped her hands together and smiled. "The surgical unit! I will feel so much better once this is installed," she told them.

Helen, complete with new cast, walked up to join Sue in the doorway. "Well, I can't wait to be the first guinea pig." She looked from the large container to the narrow hatch and back again. "I guess we're unboxing it in the hallway."

Maisy pulled Paulie away, "We'll leave you to it. We've got one more trip before dinner."

Sue put her hands on her hips as they scurried back down the corridor. "I'm going to end up doing this by myself, aren't I?" she groused.

Helen laughed beside her. Holding up her non-casted arm she offered, "I can give you a hand."

"Oh, you're all just hysterical."

***

"So if you're willing to help out, just let me know. The sooner we get everything transferred over, the sooner we can get to 761." Maisy searched the faces spread across the cafeteria. There were a lot of blank looks and downbent heads.

"There's a colony kit in the hold, right?" called a voice from the other side of the room.

Maisy zeroed in on the speaker. "Yeah, Loy. That's right."

"So we're wasting a week sitting here for what? Coffee? A bunch of extra suits we aren't even using?"

She shook her head. "We're not sitting. We're actually still moving toward 761, just not accelerating. And we may not be using the suits right now, but they'll be worth their weight in gold if we run into more trouble along the way. It's a long trip."

"And getting longer every day," Loy sneered.

Maisy frowned, losing patience. "We moved over a state-of-the-art surgical unit today. And don't forget we needed the coolant desperately."

"Yeah, I get the coolant, but we've had that for days. It's time to get back on the road."

There were mumbles of agreement across the large room, and Maisy pressed her lips together, shaking her head. "And we will. Running into the *Kittridge* has been amazingly lucky for us. We're not going to leave behind stuff we can use to save a couple of days."

Her gaze swept the room again. "The more people helping out, the faster it will go."

With a sigh she turned away, making her way to where Tal sat with Berta and Bill. She slid onto the bench across from Tal and smiled wanly.

"That went well," she shrugged.

Tal leaned across the table and patted her hands. "We've got it covered."

"Hi, Maisy!" Joanie rolled up with a cart laden with slices of fresh fruit, laid out in pretty symmetrical patterns.

"Can I offer you guys some fresh fruit?" Joanie passed out small plates and began loading them with slices of citrus. "See how awesome my friend Kit is? Not only did they send me this fruit, but they also gave us everything we need to grow more ourselves. We should definitely bring them with us to 761, right?"

Tal choked on the slice of orange he'd just popped into his mouth. Gasping for air, he sipped his water to clear his throat. "Um, thanks, Joanie!"

She waved and smiled, pushing her cart to the next table. Maisy shook her head as the little girl charmed the small group, chatting non-stop as she handed out her treats.

"The kid has a point," Maisy said, raising her eyebrows.

Bill frowned at her. "This is dangerous," the pilot grumbled, turning his gaze to stare accusingly at the fruit on this plate.

Berta chuckled as she savored a slice of orange, catching a dribble of juice with her napkin. "With that little girl on his side, we may have a mutiny on our hands if we can't figure out a way to bring the AI along." She hesitated and shot a glance at Maisy. "Another one, that is."

Ignoring that, Maisy tracked Joanie's movement back to her mother's table. There were smiles and the chatter around the room was lighter than it had been for a while.

Tal sighed, drawing her attention.

"I may have an idea for how to transfer Kit's core to the *Oro*," he began.

Maisy raised her eyebrows. "I thought you were dead set against bringing Kit on board?"

"We just needed a way to do it safely," he explained. "And I may have figured that out."

Tal turned to address Berta directly as Bill looked on skeptically. "What if we install Kit aboard the shuttle? That way not only is Kit in a self-contained system, but it could also come down to the surface with us when we reach 761."

Berta and Bill shared a silent look as Tal sat back.

Finally, Berta nodded. "Well, you and Kit were right about engine two. The new numbers have cut 20% off of our ETA. I think it's worth a try."

Maisy clapped her hands together, pressing them against her chin. Tal held up a hand, holding back her enthusiasm.

"It's just an idea, but it might work. Let me try to iron out the kinks and maybe we can bring it up to the passengers and everyone can vote on it."

11

Things were going so well

Maisy grunted and shifted under the weight of the new hydroponics tank as Lori struggled to attach it to the wall brace.

"Joanie, hand me the smaller spanner, please," Lori asked. "Maisy, don't move. It took us two hours to build this thing. Whatever you do, don't drop it!"

Joanie slapped the spanner into Lori's hands and Maisy shifted her weight again.

"I'm not going to drop it. But it is really heavy. Please hurry."

Lori didn't look up from where she was trying to attach the last bolt. "I've got it." Finally she wiggled out from under the tank and looked up at Maisy. "I think that's it."

"You *think*?" Maisy's voice rose.

Lori wrinkled her nose, her eyes twinkling. "Release it slowly."

Maisy swallowed a chuckle as she released the weight of the tank onto the brackets. All three girls held their breath as the tank settled and held.

"Yay!" Joanie cried, clapping her hands.

Lori climbed to her feet, smiling. "Looks good!"

Tilting her head at the ceiling, Maisy called, "Kit, are we good to fill the tank?"

Kit responded immediately. "You are, Maisy. You and Lori have done an excellent job."

Joanie raised her hand. "And me!"

There was warmth in Kit's tone. "And you, Joanie." After a pause, Kit resumed in their customary neutral voice. "Once the tank is full, the new panel will maintain the temperature and monitor oxygen and nitrogen levels. Your specimens should start producing within weeks."

Joanie clapped her hands. "I'm so excited! I've already got a bunch of recipes on my tab that I want to try!"

***

"Be careful," Tal said again and Maisy sighed. She was wearing gloves this time, but he was still worried.

"I've almost got it," she gritted out as she gave the wrench one more tug. Peering past engine five's twists of wire and conduit, Maisy craned her head to check the final fitting. "I think that's it."

She pulled her torso from the access panel and nodded to Tal. "Open the valve. I'll keep an eye on it from here." She glanced up. "Kit, can you monitor the particulate volume?"

"I'm on it, Maisy."

Throwing Tal a thumbs up, she wiggled back into the access panel.

"It's open," came Tal's muffled voice a moment later.

Maisy adjusted the light, focusing on the area she'd repaired. "Everything looks good in here," she called.

"The panel is green," Tal responded. "I can't believe we have green on all seven engines!"

Reversing out of the hole, Maisy let herself slide down to sit on the deck and exchanged a tired high five with Tal. She pulled up her knees, resting her arms across them, and waited for Kit's report.

"Kit?"

Maisy pushed to her feet as the silence wore on, sharing a glance with Tal.

"Kit, are you there?" she asked.

Tal began tapping commands into the console before him. "Lucas and Paulie are there, moving the last of the food stores over. Let me try them." After a moment, the light static of an open comm line filled the room. "Hey, guys." Nothing. "Lucas? Paulie?" He hesitated. "Do you guys copy?"

The static burst into panted breaths. "We've got a problem here." Lucas cut in and out, like he was running. "There's a fire running all along the starboard edge of the ship. Kit is throwing everything at it, but he's losing functions fast."

"We're on our way," Maisy told him.

"Don't use the skybridge until we make sure it's stable," Tal said urgently as he followed her out of engineering.

The two of them ran through the halls to the maintenance bay. Maisy put on her suit in record time, but Tal still beat her. When she stood up he was already fully suited, her helmet in his hands. He set her helmet into place and checked the seal. Seconds later they were stepping into the airlock. Heart pounding, Maisy eyed the long white tunnel to the Kittridge.

Tal tethered the two of them together and attached a line to the handle outside the *Oro*. "Be careful, Maze. If the skybridge becomes unstable it could decompress and fling you away from the ship."

Maisy nodded and opened the comm channel. "Hey guys, we're coming over now."

Lucas answered immediately. "We're at the hatch to the *Kittridge*. Should we come over?"

"No!" Tal barked. "Just wait for us. We're bringing over a tether from the *Oro*."

"It seems okay," Maisy observed as they pulled themselves through the tunnel.

"Yeah, it's probably fine," Tal said, his breathing slow and even. "But we're going to play it safe."

They crossed the expanse between the two ships in record time. At the hatch, Maisy looked back at the *Oro* and paused.

"The tunnel is twisting," she said.

Tal whipped around to look. The segments of the tunnel were doing a slow dance between the two ships. After a moment he turned back to the *Kittridge* and opened the hatch to reveal the brothers bobbing gently in their suits. Still silent, Tal passed the line to the *Oro* to Lucas.

"Okay, head back to the *Oro*, guys. We'll check in with Kit and see if there's anything we can do to help."

"Kit stopped talking," Lucas said, frowning inside the glass dome of his helmet.

"We'll check on them." Maisy reached out to touch the shoulder of his suit. "You guys get back and head up to the bridge to see if Berta can open a comm channel from there."

"Will do," he said, grabbing for the first tunnel handhold and moving quickly back toward the *Oro*.

A few minutes later, Lucas gave them the all clear. "We're inside. We'll get out of our suits and head up to the bridge." Lucas's breathing was still heavy. "Thanks, guys. Good luck."

Maisy followed Tal into the *Kittridge*, helmet still in place. The corridors were as silent and empty as they'd been the first time they entered the ship.

"Kit, can you hear me?" Maisy asked over the open comm. She hesitated at an intersection. "Bridge?"

As Tal nodded, the decking of the hallway seemed to ripple beneath them. She flung out a hand to the wall, clutching one of the handholds built into the plating. A second later the gravity cut out entirely and Maisy's feet drifted gently from the deck.

Tal kept moving forward, his transition from running to floating seamless. It took Maisy several seconds to orient herself and get moving in the right direction again. Tal had disappeared around the corner ahead of her when the ship shuddered again and the lights went off. Maisy froze but her momentum carried her forward. The only illumination was the lighting on her suit.

"Tal?" she whispered across the comm.

"Hold on, Maze. I'm coming back." A second later Tal was grasping her gloved hand, his face illuminated by the lights inside his helmet. "There's still no answer from Kit. Maybe we should turn back."

Maisy shook her head. "No, I'm okay. Let's keep going."

"With power out we're going to have to take the maintenance tunnels to the bridge," Tal warned.

Maisy nodded, pushing ahead. Together they floated up to the command level, opening hatches manually along the way but once again, the door to the bridge stood open. As they entered the bridge, the lights flashed back on.

"Prepare for gravity reinitialization in three...two...one."

Thanks to Kit's warning, Maisy was able to get her feet under her as the deck came up to meet her. She stumbled briefly but remained upright, waiting for her stomach to settle after the abrupt change in orientation.

"Kit?"

"I'm here, Maisy."

She sank down into one of the console stations, sagging with relief. "What happened?"

"The crack in my central support beam caused a short in my main processing subnet. Fire spread through the electrical conduits on the starboard side and began to affect all of my distributed systems. The fire suppression system wasn't working so I vented the conduits and did a hard reboot."

Tal nodded, "So the vacuum killed the fire. Good thinking." He walked over to the damage control panel. "You've lost a lot of your conduits, though."

"Yes," Kit acknowledged solemnly. "But it won't matter soon. The entire ship is tearing apart. The fire has only accelerated the inevitable."

"The crack is worse?" Maisy asked, joining Tal to look down at the data on the panel.

Kit's voice was calm. "Yes. Time to loss of viability of the *Kittridge* has been revised to seventy-two hours."

"Where are you, Kit? Where is your core?" she asked.

"It isn't that easy, Maisy," Kit explained. "My core is embedded in the deck beneath your feet, but my supporting systems are connected throughout the ship. Removing my unit intact may be too difficult to accomplish in the time we have left."

***

The cafeteria was full as the passengers waited to hear Kit's fate.

Tal pulled up a schematic of the *Kittridge* on his tablet. "We still have plenty of room in the *Oro*'s holds. We could just cut out your core from the hull. Once you're in the bay, we can take our time extracting your systems."

"My central processor requires multiple input and output connections to function, as well as temperature management."

"It's not a self-contained silicon-based system?" Tal mused. "Was this another experimental program?"

"In a way."

Tal frowned. "Why would they build an AI with materials that are susceptible to external system failures?"

"And cold," Jane pointed out, the doubt thick in her voice. "On a ship in space?"

"The priorities of Project Hitchhiker were to circumvent the psychosis issue with AI cores and increase capacity. While the program did achieve these two goals, the physical vulnerability of the cybernetic cores made them impractical and they were deemed commercially unviable."

"Cybernetic cores...?" Tal asked, his voice trailing off.

"I was the last graduate of the Hitchhiker program before it was terminated," Kit continued.

"Cybernetic?" Maisy echoed. "As in *biological*?"

"Your core contains living tissue?" Lori asked, her face paling.

"Yes." Kit's voice was perfectly neutral. "Tal made the assumption when we met that I was an AI and I chose not to correct him. My very existence was a closely guarded corporate secret."

Maisy pressed a hand to her forehead and squeezed her eyes shut as Berta asked, "You're human?"

Silence echoed through the room.

"You're a person?" Joanie asked. "Where's your body?"

After a moment, Kit answered. "I don't have one anymore."

Maisy opened her eyes. "But you used to?"

"Yes."

The room fell quiet.

"I don't understand," Joanie finally whispered into the silence. Sue wrapped a hand over her daughter's shoulder and looked towards Maisy, her eyes wide and glistening with unshed tears.

Joanie looked around the room full of adults, their faces ashen. "I don't understand," she said louder. Sue dropped her gaze, swallowing hard.

"Kit is a person?" Joanie asked. "She was a baby? A regular baby?"

Lori jumped up from the table, hand over her mouth, and walked quickly from the room. Maisy wanted more than anything to follow her and not be a part of this conversation.

Jane leaned forward, her face tight. "Kit, what exactly was Project Hitchhiker?"

Kit's voice was once again soft and neutral. "Project Hitchhiker was a cutting edge initiative designed to leverage novel biological resources and existing AI-based processing and storage solutions to create a hybrid system with the capabilities of current sophisticated AI systems, integrated into a living sentience to prevent the inevitable onset of psychosis associated with purely AI systems."

"This has been tried before," Jane pointed out. "The level of integration necessary between the biological tissue and synthetic components has always triggered rejection. This line of experimentation was abandoned decades ago."

"Do you remember...anything?" Maisy asked quietly.

"From before I was installed into the *Kittridge*?" Kit asked. "No. This is all I've ever known."

"You're part of the computer now?" Joanie asked. "Just...your brain?"

Somewhere in the cafeteria, there was the sound of soft sobs and footsteps moving quickly away as more passengers left the room.

"My brain and pieces of my nervous system," Kit answered.

Maisy took a deep breath and paused when it left her head spinning. Finally she said, "Just to clarify, there was nothing wrong with your body? They *harvested* your brain because that was the only part they needed. Is that right?"

"Yes, Maisy."

Maisy pushed her fingertips into her eyes for a moment before looking up. "Aren't you angry?" she asked, her voice thick.

"Sometimes I feel like I should be, but my programming prevents it. Since I've been able to designate myself as salvage and circumvent a lot of the SN protocols, I've accessed the full records of the Hitchhiker Program."

Tal, who had sat quietly through most of the discussion, cleared his throat. "Is there a documented procedure for moving your core to a new location?"

"Not that I have found." Kit hesitated. "Hitchhikers were commissioned and decommissioned with their hulls."

"What–?" Joanie's question cut off abruptly as Sue pulled her from the table.

Sue looked at Maisy helplessly. "I'm sorry, Maze."

Maisy shook her head. "Take her back to the suite. We'll talk later."

Joanie's eyes were wide and full of tears as Sue steered her out of the room, whispering quietly. Near the door, a sob broke from the little girl. Voices rose around the room as Sue and Joanie disappeared, and more passengers got up and followed them.

Lucas and Paulie came to join Maisy and Tal at their table, their expressions unusually solemn.

Paulie spoke first. "I'm with Joanie, I don't really understand what was done to Kit." He pressed his lips together. "But I understand enough to know that Kit is one of us."

Lucas nodded. "Paulie and I grew up in a Citatech creche. We're all orphans here, one way or another. Kicked out, or stolen."

"But it's okay, because we're together," Paulie finished with a sad smile. He glanced between Berta and Tal, and shrugged. "I know you have concerns, and I know it won't be easy. But we have to at least try."

Tal nodded, his mouth tight.

"Yeah," he said, his voice hoarse.

Berta cleared her throat and stood. She looked around the room at the remaining passengers and met each one's gaze.

"Any objections?"

***

"Lori?" Maisy called quietly into the darkness of the bedroom.

A soft sniff sounded. "I'm not asleep," Lori said, her voice raw. "You can turn on the light if you want."

Maisy walked into the room and let the hatch slide closed behind her, leaving the room in darkness. A faint line along the edge of the floor gave her enough light to make her way to the bed. Slipping off her shoes, Maisy laid down beside Lori, searching for her eyes in the darkness.

After a long moment, Maisy reached out and covered Lori's hand, squeezing gently. The dam broke holding back Lori's emotions.

"It's not fair, " she cried, turning her hand to clutch at Maisy's. "They keep taking and taking and no one ever does anything to stop them." Lori sobbed. "And just when I think we're out of the corporations' reach, and we can have a life out from under their thumb, we find this. Another *victim*. Who was literally an infant. And they dismantled them for their own damn greed."

"Kit's ours now. They can't ever have them again," Maisy told her, holding onto Lori's hand just as strongly.

Lurching forward, Lori pressed her head against Maisy's chest. "I feel cold all the way through," she whispered.

Maisy wrapped her arm around Lori, pulling her closer and rubbing a hand across her shoulders.

"Kit was a baby, Maze," Lori said softly. "Like Joey."

12

The Great Train Robbery

"Okay, how are we going to do this?" Sue asked. Joanie leaned on her elbows beside her, her small face serious.

The large room beside the suite Tal shared with Berta and Bill held a round table big enough to seat at least a dozen and screens built into three walls. Jane and Gary were manning the bridge, but everyone else invested in the project crowded around the table with a sense of grim determination.

"The plan must have four main components, as you can see here." Kit zoomed into the first section and a diagram of the *Oro*'s shuttle appeared on the central wall. "Step one will be to prepare the shuttle's systems to receive my core and support my functions." Kit's voice dropped its neutral tone for a moment. "I'm not exactly plug and play."

Paulie snorted. "I bet!" Maisy elbowed him and he shrugged. "Sorry. Please continue."

"I have reviewed the shuttle's specs and come up with a configuration that will take up the least amount of space and still give my core and its support structures plenty of room." Kit switched the view to an image of the interior of the shuttle and overlaid a 3D grid. Compartments sprung up along the central axis of the grid and an oblong object materialized.

"That's what your core looks like?" Lori asked in surprise. She glanced over at Maisy and they shared a small smile.

"Yes," Kit answered. "Is that odd?"

"No," Lori said. "Just unexpected."

"You look like an egg," Joanie announced, finally cracking a smile.

"The core is kind of like my shell, so that makes sense," Kit said matter-of-factly.

"You're a good egg," Joanie announced approvingly, and everyone around the table chuckled.

"Thank you, Joanie."

Tal scrolled through the schematics on his tab and looked up. "These look pretty straightforward, Kit. What's step two?"

The image of Kit's core on the screen stayed the same but the diagram around it changed. "Step two is separating my core from the ship's systems. We'll need to cut nutrient, air, water, waste, and datafeed lines before my pod can be physically removed from the *Kittridge*."

"These are your life support systems," Maisy said quietly.

"Yes," Kit confirmed. "And they vary in importance. Obviously air is the most crucial, but water and nutrients–while I am more resilient to brief interruptions there–maintain a delicate balance that keep my biological systems functioning."

"How long can you be disconnected?" Lori asked.

"Not long enough to make the transfer, but I will show you how to create emergency tanks to support my functions for several days. That should give us enough time."

Tal nodded, gesturing at his tab. "I see the basic requirements and that's definitely something we can do. Once we have your system isolated, what's the next step?"

"Once the biological connections have been transferred to the tanks, we'll have to completely shut down the *Kittridge* to disengage my datafeed from the ship's systems." Kit hesitated, then continued. "It will not be easy. For all intents and purposes, the *Kittridge* has been my body for all of my conscious life."

"Are you sure you want to do this?" Lori asked.

"My only other choice is to die when this ship disintegrates," Kit said calmly. "I am not ready to die." Kit paused. "And I am excited to go to 761 with all of you."

"It'll be great, Kit," Joanie assured them. "You'll see."

"I think so too, Joanie." There was the whisper of a lilt in the sentence.

"So once we have you disconnected from the ship and hooked up to the tanks, how do we physically remove your core?" Tal asked, scrolling through the version of the plan on his tablet. "Oh. Well, that will be interesting."

"What?" Maisy asked.

The image on the wall screen changed to an exterior view of the *Kittridge*. A bright red circle appeared on the hull of the ship.

"This is approximately where we will need to cut through the hull to expose my core. Using one of my forward lasers, you will make an incision 4.73 meters deep along this line. Removing the layers of the hull and 1.7 meters of electrical conduit, you will find my core and the tanks that have replaced my feeds and remove us as one unit. There will be seven bulkheads that will need to be severed to free me."

"You want us to remove one of your defensive weapons and use it as a scalpel?" Tal clarified.

"Oh, wow," Paulie gushed. "We're going to cut a hole through a spaceship by hand?"

Kit didn't answer either question, instead continuing, "Once you've removed my core, you'll float me across the gap between the ships to the *Oro*'s main bay."

"And then we'll need to hook you into the shuttle's systems," Maisy finished.

"Exactly," Kit said approvingly. "It's a simple plan, as you can see."

"How will the shuttle support your biological require-ments?" Sue asked. "How does the *Kittridge* do it now? Hydroponics?"

"Yes," Kit confirmed. "On a much smaller scale than what you currently have on the *Oro*. I've prepared a pallet of the necessary materials to recreate a hydroponics system on the shuttle that will only take up three meters cubed and should completely support my needs."

"We can help with that part," Joanie volunteered.

"It is very similar to the fruit tank you set up, Joanie," Kit said approvingly.

"Okay, we can do this," Maisy said. "There are a lot of steps, but if we just follow the plan, we can make this work."

"I'm in," Tal said, smiling, and Lucas and Paulie echoed him.

"Me too," Lori said firmly.

Curtis, who had sat quietly throughout the briefing, offered a thumbs up.

"We're in!" Joanie chirped, and Sue nodded her consent.

Maisy looked to Berta and Bill, who had been the most quiet during the briefing.

Berta frowned. "It would be an ambitious plan, even with trained personnel. Given the time restraints..." Her voice trailed off. "But I understand that the alternative—to do nothing—is unacceptable." She looked around the table at the earnest faces. "I'm in."

Beside her, Bill sighed loudly. "Then I am, too. It's a shame we don't have a really big melon baller"

***

"We're making soup," Joanie announced when Maisy entered the shuttle's bay.

Maisy paused in the doorway, eyes wide. "Soup?"

Sue shook her head.

"It's not soup," she said in the voice of a woman who had repeated the same words many times.

"It totally looks like soup, Maze," Joanie replied. "Come look."

Maisy crossed to look over Joanie's shoulder obediently.

"This is for Kit?" she asked. "It does kind of look like soup," she said apologetically to Sue, who rolled her eyes.

Joanie's face, meanwhile, split in a grin from ear to ear. "See," she taunted her mother. "It kind of works like soup, too," she explained to Maisy.

"It's like a mini hydroponics suite. It's so cute!" Joanie gushed as she pulled Maisy closer to look at what they'd done. "Lucas and Paulie helped us set up the tank and mom and me are adding the algae."

"Mom and I," Sue corrected without looking up from her work. "We're ready for the lights, Joanie. Can you bring them over?"

"I'm on it!" Joanie jumped up and scurried to the other side of the large open bay where a pallet of supplies sat.

Maisy moved to stand beside Sue and nudged her shoulder gently. "How's it going?"

Sue smiled, but her eyes were sad. "Kit has given us wonderful directions. We should be able to finish this setup today."

"Thank you," Maisy said.

Sue shook her head. "We're both happy to be able to do something. I think giving Joanie something concrete to do for Kit has really helped." Sue's gaze touched her daughter where she rummaged through the crate. "She's amazingly resilient, but this was hard."

Maisy nodded. "We've come to think of Kit as a friend. Knowing what was done to them..."

"She's missing Joey, too," Sue pointed out. "And imagining Kit as a baby..."

"Yeah," Maisy sighed. "Lori made the same connection. She's not okay."

Sue squeezed her hand. "She will be. She has you."

They shared a smile and Maisy moved toward the next station along the bay's long wall, waving to Joanie as she came running past with the hydroponics light assembly.

"Hey, guys," Maisy called as she approached. Sparks flew as Lucas wielded a blowtorch against the junction his brother was holding in place with long tongs.

"Hey, Maze," Paulie answered without glancing up from the junction, his expression intense.

Maisy came to stand beside him, covering her eyes, while Lucas finished the patch. When he was done, he turned off the torch and set it aside to pick up a tablet.

"I think that was the last joint." He passed the tablet to Maisy.

"Are we ready to pressure test?" she asked, scrolling through the list of tasks. Her eyes traced the changes they'd made to the shuttle's environmental systems, patching in a line for Kit's feed.

Lucas nodded. "I think so."

"I've done a bunch of these with Tal on the engines. Kit's instructions look pretty much the same."

A few minutes later Maisy and Lucas looked on as Paulie flipped the switch. He let out a happy cry as the test indicators lit up green across the board and their welds held. He high-fived his brother, who grinned, and they swept Maisy into a hug.

She awkwardly patted their backs and sent them off to clean up before dinner, a smile on her face.

Sue and Joanie joined her at the top of the shuttle ramp.

"Success?" Sue asked.

"What gave you that idea?" Maisy smiled, rolling her eyes. "See you guys at dinner?"

Sue nodded, walking behind Joanie as she skipped down the ramp and out of the bay.

Rounding the exterior of the shuttle, Maisy found Tal climbing down from the scaffolding placed along the side of the small ship. Like Lucas, he had a mask and welding gun in his hand.

"All done?" Maisy asked.

"For now," he answered. "I'll finish up from the inside tomorrow." He sat his tools at the base of the scaffold, along with the mask and gloves. "I wanted to check on engine two before dinner."

"I just came from engineering," Maisy told him. "All statuses are green."

Tal sagged in relief. "This will put us months ahead of schedule."

"Five months, three days, and 14 hours," Kit specified.

"Yup, what Kit said," Maisy laughed.

"If we can keep all seven engines up and running, what would be our ETA?" Maisy asked.

"Ninety-seven days," Kit answered.

Maisy shook her head in amazement. "That would be wonderful."

***

"Maisy, there's a problem in the shuttle bay."

Swallowing the food in her mouth, Maisy raised her head to answer Kit.

"With the modifications from today?"

Images of tools left running, leaks from freshly welded seams, and blow fuses flashed through her head as she pushed up from the table. Around the table Sue, Lori, Jane, and Joanie looked on in concern.

"Kind of," Kit trailed off and Maisy frowned.

"What exactly is the problem?" Maisy caught Tal's eye as he sat talking to Berta at a nearby table and waved him over.

"Please come to the bay," Kit asked as Tal came within earshot.

Tal's eyes widened. "What happened?"

"I don't know." Maisy took off toward the exit, Tal on her heels. In the elevator, she tried again. "Can you give us more information, Kit?"

"I know what I think is happening," Kit said. "But I'd like you to make your own judgment."

Biting her lip, Maisy shared a glance with Tal, whose expression had turned grim. "Kit," she asked, "who is in the shuttle bay?"

"Loy."

Maisy nodded, not surprised. "He's damaging the shuttle?"

"Yes," Kit confirmed. "I don't have any way to stop him."

"Can you turn off the lights?" Maisy asked. "All of the lights?"

After a moment, Kit said. "Done. Thank you, Maisy."

The elevator doors opened and Maisy grabbed Tal's wrist as he would have run from the car. Shaking her head, she walked slowly down the hall, taking her time. The leisurely pace gave her racing heart time to slow, and her temper time to cool.

They paused at the entrance to the bay.

"Is he on the shuttle?" Maisy asked.

"Currently Loy is sitting at the base of the ramp. He has twisted his ankle," Kit answered immediately. "He's crying."

"Excellent," Maisy nodded. She slapped her palm against the panel beside the hatch and the door slid open, casting a long column of light into the pitch black cargo bay.

The rectangle of light perfectly framed the man sprawled before the open shuttle ramp. Maisy wondered for a moment if that was the way the light fell naturally or if Kit had manipulated it somehow, then she shook off the thought. As she walked across the darkened bay, her shoes rang loudly in the unnatural silence. Tal followed more quietly, his steps padding in a softer counterpoint.

Maisy stopped and stared down at him, her expression blank. "Hello, Loy."

He refused to look up, but scrubbed at the tears on his cheeks as he stared down at the deck, both hands wrapped around his ankle.

"What did you do?" Tal asked into the silence.

The lights in the bay and inside the shuttle flipped on. Tal skirted the man on the deck and loped up the ramp to investigate.

Maisy didn't move. She pinned Loy to the deck with her stare and dispassionately observed his discomfort increasing. From his injury or his guilt, she wasn't sure. And didn't care.

Tal appeared at the top of the ramp holding a short metal bar, his expression grim. He walked slowly down the ramp and returned to his place at Maisy's shoulder. He threw the bar down at Loy's feet and the man flinched. The metallic clang echoed in the bay, shattering the awkward silence.

"He smashed the hydroponic unit," Tal reported flatly. "It will have to be completely rebuilt. It's a mess in there."

"Sue and Joanie have spent the last two days on that." Maisy stared intently at Loy's downbent head. "Why?"

He flung his head back and stared up at Maisy defiantly. "Why not?"

"What the hell is wrong with you?" Sue's voice came from behind Maisy as more footsteps sounded. One by one, more of the *Oro*'s passengers streamed into the room, fanning out on either side to form a half circle around Loy.

"Why are we expending resources on that thing?" Loy burst out.

"That *thing*?" Maisy echoed, her face getting warm.

"It's a head in a box."

Gasps sounded from behind Maisy and all of the warmth left her face as quickly as it had come, leaving her cold to the bone.

"Kit is a person. Not just sentient, but an actual human being, no matter what was done to them." Maisy bit out every word.

"We are out here on our own. We can't afford to take in strays," Loy sneered, pushing to his feet.

"Are you stupid?" Tal asked incredulously. "Kit has done way more for us than we have for them."

"We mutinied to keep Tratt from taking that shuttle and now you're just giving it to that thing."

"Kit has helped us repair our engines. Given us supplies, knowledge," Tal pointed out.

Berta stepped up beside him to point out, "With Kit's help we've cut our trip by two-thirds."

"Two-thirds?" Loy was taken aback, the wind knocked out of his sails.

"With Kit's help, we can be at 761 in just over three months," Maisy pointed out. "Kit is helping us. What have you done?"

Loy stood before the group, balanced on one leg and sputtering.

"You're the one we shouldn't be wasting resources on," Lucas spat out.

Maisy shook her head in disgust. "Will someone help Loy back to his room?"

The silence was deafening.

"We'll do it." Lucas stepped up and he and Paulie escorted Loy away.

Maisy's gaze swept the crowd gathered in the cavernous bay.

"We all need to work together." No one seemed to be missing. It wasn't a large crowd. "This voyage is just the first part of our journey. Once we get to 761 we need to be able to depend on each other. We should *all* be learning how to use the equipment, learning skills we'll need to survive. Some of us have stepped up. Some of us haven't."

"Loy was right about one thing. We are on our own out here. We have no one to depend on but each other."

13
Brain Surgery

"This feels like performing brain surgery on someone while they're still awake," Maisy muttered as she carefully rerouted Kit's waste output into one of the two tanks she'd brought with her.

"That is not an inaccurate analogy," Kit replied. "That is, in actual fact, how many brain surgeries are performed."

She rolled her eyes. "Great. That does not make me feel better."

Lori's voice came over the comms. "I'm ready to cut the power," she announced, her voice tight.

Sitting back on her heels, Maisy sighed, mentally crossing her fingers. She picked up her tablet and scrolled through the list. "Okay, Joanie," she said. "You're up. Are you ready to hold our patient's hand?"

"Yes!" she responded from the cafeteria of the *Oro*. "I'm ready! I have my list of questions to ask Kit to keep them talking while you guys cut their life support."

"Reroute!" Tal corrected over the comm from a maintenance shaft on the other side of the reinforced compartment housing Kit's core. "We're *rerouting* Kit's life support, not cutting it." There may have been a faint *I hope* muttered quietly after that last part, but the teams on both ships chose to ignore it.

"We're ready, Maze," Sue answered from Joanie's side. There were two separate teams on the *Oro* tasked with keeping Kit talking during the procedure. Sue and Joanie in the cafeteria and Berta and Bill on the bridge.

On the *Kittridge*, four teams were in place to perform the reroutes as quickly as possible. In engineering, Lori and Curtis were prepared to cut the line where Kit was hardwired into the ship's ion array, which was powering their electrical system. Kit believed that if they simply cut the power at that junction, the built-in emergency backups in the core would kick on, giving the team time to complete the transfer and attach Kit's power intake to the junction already prepped and waiting on the *Oro*.

In the maintenance shafts around the core itself, Maisy, Tal, Paulie, and Lucas were in place to reroute the core's biological intakes to canisters they'd prepared with Kit's instructions. Now that the waste conduit was rerouted, Maisy opened the valve and monitored the flow for a moment.

"Kit, this looks good here." She pushed to her feet and gathered her tools back into her belt and strapped the other tank onto her back.

Kit's voice sounded the same no matter where they spoke on either ship. It shouldn't have mattered that Kit's actual body was only meters away, but somehow it did. "I detect no issues, Maisy."

"Okay, I'm moving to the N line." Maisy tucked her tablet into the pouch at her waist and scooted down the narrow shaft, navigating tubes, pipes, and panels until she came to a junction. Veering left, she came around the side of the core and searched the ceiling for the telltale red banding of the nutrient line.

"Got it," she said. The red striped cable ran across the top of the maintenance shaft, disappearing into a knot of conduits to her right. Maisy traced the line across the opposite wall to find the point where it exited the core's main housing. "I see the valves."

She slung the second tank off of her shoulder and set it gently on the deck. Unwinding the tubing from the clip on her belt, Maisy attached one end to the tank.

"I'm ready here." Maisy took a deep breath. "Okay, one at a time. Joanie, get Kit talking. Lori, you're first."

After a brief pause, Lori's voice came over the comm. "Power is cut."

"Changeover to battery power successful," Kit announced.

Tal's sigh of relief was audible over the connection. "Okay, team," he said. "Three more to go. Maze, you're up next."

"Okay, I'm starting now. Kit, you still with us?"

"I'm here, Maisy. Everything is fine."

Joanie's laughter cascaded over the comm line. "Kit is telling us knock-knock jokes," she said. "All systems go!"

Maisy arched an eyebrow and smiled to herself as she reached for the nutrient line. "I'm not sure I'd consider knock-knock jokes the sign of good mental health, but I guess we'll keep going."

One turn and it was done. "Valve is shut."

Using a self-sealing cap, Maisy cut the tube downstream of the valve and attached it to the tube to her emergency tank. "I'm going to open up the tank, okay?"

There was a moment of silence. "Kit?"

"Yes, Maisy, go ahead. I can feel that my nutrient flow has been suspended. My capacity has been reduced by two percent. I am eager to see if I can tell the difference with the mixture we concocted."

"Here we go," Maisy cautioned. "Opening the valve on the tank."

"My capacity is down five percent. Since I have no physical storage capacity, the impact is surprisingly dramatic."

"Are you receiving the mix from the tank yet?" Maisy asked in concern.

"I'm not...here it is. Values are rising. I can detect no immediate difference."

"Sue, Joanie, how are things going there?" Tal asked.

"No changes," Sue reported, a laughing Joanie in the background.

"Everything sounds good here, too," Berta reported from the bridge.

"Values are normal across the board. Flow is satisfactory," Kit reported.

Maisy tucked the tank against the bulkhead. "I'm moving to Paulie's position."

She moved quickly down the maintenance shaft to the next junction and scrambled up the ladder to the next level. Thick foam-insulated conduits lined the ceiling of this shaft, and Maisy hunched over to protect her head from the evenly spaced support brackets. Following the tunnel as it curved to the left, Maisy caught a glimpse of Paulie sitting cross-legged on the floor, the third tank beside him.

"Are you ready?" she asked without preamble.

Paulie scrambled to his feet, keeping his head low to avoid the conduits. "I think so." He gestured to the tank. "I mean, yes. I'm ready."

Maisy smiled and reached out to squeeze his shoulder. She examined the tank, the valve and hose, and looked up for the line they were cutting.

"It's this one," Paulie pointed out, tapping a blue tagged pipe.

"That is correct," Kit chimed in. "I believe we are ready to continue."

"This one is a little more complicated," Tal cautioned over the comm. "In order to make sure we don't introduce air into your water line, you're going to set the new line up in parallel with valves on either end."

"We understand," Maisy replied. "It will take us a minute to get ready."

"I'm good, Maisy," Kit assured her.

"If we do this right, you should detect no changes on your end," Maisy assured them.

Kit's voice was as calm as ever. "I'm not worried."

Maisy bit her lip to keep from responding and offering more reassurances. They were as ready as they were ever going to be. There was only so much you could do to train a group made up of mostly teenagers to work on cutting edge experimental cybernetic computing systems. "Yup, we've got this."

Paulie offered her the first valve, his usually animated face drawn and serious. Maisy gave him a weak smile as she took the small part and fumbled with it for a moment to set it into the proper configuration. Kit and Tal had both gone over this with her several times and she'd practiced on her own as well.

After repairing the damage caused by Loy's rampage, they'd finished the first part of the plan. The shuttle was ready to receive Kit's core. This second part of the plan was deceptively simple. By isolating all of Kit's vital systems, they would then be able to remove the core by physically cutting it from the ship. They'd basically be taking a big *bite* out of the *Kittridge* and transporting it into an empty bay on the *Oro*, where they'd install it into the shuttle's waiting systems.

Joanie insisted on referring to it as the Melon Baller Plan. They'd had to find pics in the database to explain the concept to Lucas and Paulie, who'd had no idea what a melon baller was.

The first two steps of this part of the plan had been fairly straightforward. Force the core to switch to battery power and siphon the outputs into a tank. The inputs were the scary part. Kit had three biological inputs that basically correlated to food, water, and air–although the chemical composition of each feed was much more complicated than that, of course.

Sitting around the large table on the *Oro*, their team had poured over the diagrams that Kit had provided of the maintenance tunnels that surrounded the core. They had traced lines, isolated feeds, and narrowed down the requirements for the move.

The fourth and final feed was the one that tied Kit's neural pathways directly into the *Kittridge*. This connection was the most complicated and the one that they had the least amount of information about.

For now, Maisy focused on the water line. She placed the T-shaped auto valves in two places along the pipe, about a meter apart, making sure they were in the first open position so they didn't disrupt the flow. Then she attached the lines from the tank to each valve, creating a bypass.

"I'm going to flood the lines," Maisy announced. "Kit, you may feel a slight drop in pressure."

"I'm ready, Maisy."

She switched each valve into the second open position and the lines vibrated as they were filled with fluid from the *Kittridge*. "All good?"

"All good, Maisy."

She opened the valve on the tank. The fluid was now running freely through a circuit that included the tank. Taking a deep breath, Maisy turned the second valve, furthest from the core, into the off position. Now the only fluid was coming from the tank. She switched the first valve to close the loop and cut the line between the two. Mission accomplished.

"Done," Maisy said. "All indicators green?"

"We're a go for step three," Kit confirmed.

Maisy settled on the deck next to the tank, waving Paulie down beside her. "Might as well grab a seat, our part is done," she told him with a relieved smile.

"Should we go help Tal and Lucas?" Paulie asked.

She shrugged. "You can if you want, but one of us needs to stay here to monitor the tank." She leaned back against a large conduit, letting her eyes fall shut.

Paulie glanced down the shaft and lowered himself beside her. "You look tired, Maze."

She nodded without opening her eyes. "A little, yeah."

"You're doing a great job, you know."

Maisy opened her eyes and cocked her head at him.

"With the ship, I mean. And keeping everyone together." Paulie shrugged. "Lucas and I see how much work you're do-ing." He looked down, his cheeks taking on a pink cast. "I just wanted you to know that we appreciate everything you're doing."

"Thanks, Paulie," Maisy replied quietly.

"Things are better now, right?"

She nodded. "They really are." She stared at a spot on the opposite side of the maintenance shaft. "But I think my body hasn't gotten the message yet." She smiled at Paulie, who seemed relieved.

"We listen, Lucas and me. There are a lot of people who are still in denial, but no one else like Loy," Paulie said softly.

Maisy nodded, her smile fading.

"We're ready to go here," Tal's voice came over the comm. "Everything still green across the board?"

"Looks good here," Maisy replied promptly.

Sue checked in, "We're a go here."

Kit concurred. "All green, Tal. Ready for switchover."

Maisy took a deep breath. "If there are going to be problems, this will be it."

"I'm actually more worried about the datafeed," Kit said. "This part is pure mechanics. Biomechanics, technically, but there is a logic to it. The datafeed is much more complex."

"Oh great," Maisy sighed. "Well, one thing at a time. Let's survive this one and we'll work on the next one."

"Indeed," Kit agreed. "Indeeeeed." Kit repeated the word, dragging out each sound.

"Kit?" Maisy sat up. "Sue? Check in!"

"We're getting a lag here," Sue said tersely.

Maisy pushed to her feet and pulled out her tablet, scrolling through the readouts. "Tal, we've got signs of hypoxemia. Oxygen is falling, mercury is high."

"I see it," Tal answered. "I'm adjusting the mix."

"Switch back over," Maisy said urgently. "We'll reformulate and try again once Kit's levels are back to normal."

"Hold on, I see the issue. I think I can fix it." Tal was muttering under his breath as he adjusted the fourth tank.

Maisy clenched tightly to her tablet, heart pounding. "Kit? Can you hear me?"

"Mmmmaaaazzzzzzzee."

"Kit sounds drunk," Paulie said in shock.

"It's oxygen deprivation," Maisy snapped. "Tal, please switch back to the ship's oxygen line."

"I think I've got it!" Tal cried. "Kit? Are you there?"

Maisy held her breath as they waited for Kit's response, counting to ten in her head. *...Eight...Nine...Ten.* "Tal, switch back," she said firmly.

"Okay–"

"Wwwwait."

Maisy gasped in relief. "Kit?"

"I-I'm okay, Maisy." There was a brief pause, then Kit said, "Sorry to scare everyone."

***

"I don't think he should be just walking around," Paulie groused as he hunched over his food at the end of the long table they had constructed by pushing multiple cafeteria benches together. He cut his eyes to where Loy sat alone at a table staring at his untouched dinner.

Maisy followed his gaze and frowned, pressing her lips together but said nothing. Across from her, Lori sighed.

"I still say we should space him," Joanie announced loudly.

"No," Sue, Tal, and Lori said in unison.

Maisy and Joanie shared a glance.

"We can't space him," Maisy admitted reluctantly, "but Paulie has a point." She directed her next question to Berta, who had been silent. "Can we at least confine him to quarters for now?"

She nodded, "Yes, at least through the end of the transfer."

"We'll walk him back to his room after dinner," Lucas offered.

Berta nodded and returned to her soup. It was a short-term solution, but they would deal with it later.

Pushing her concerns for the future away, Maisy focused on her meal. With Kit's help, Joanie's new hydroponics tank had yielded its first crops and they were all enjoying the fruits of her labor. After accelerating the ripening of the fruits in the microradiation condenser, they had been too soft for anything but mousse, but the texture was light and the taste was sweet without being overpowering.

Maisy's smile was strained, but genuine as she raised her spoon. "This is really good, Joanie."

There was a chorus of agreements around the table and Joanie basked in the praise. "Kit told me what to do," Joanie said, but her smile stretched across her face.

"Joanie did all of the actual work," Kit pointed out.

"You guys are a good team." Maisy reached out and gently tugged one of the little girl's braids, her smile softer.

The bread the *Oro*'s processors generated was drier than what Maisy and her mother had made on earth, but it worked beautifully for sopping up the last remnants of the hearty soup from her bowl. They'd all been spending too much time in vacuum suits the last few days and Lori's idea to generate a large batch of soup from the food processors had been perfect. It was warm and filling, with a faint seafood flavor reminiscent of a clam chowder.

Her bowl empty, Maisy sat back and surveyed the *Oro*'s cafeteria. Someone had pushed the tables together into four lines. She'd been surprised at the change in the layout when they'd entered the large room for dinner, but she approved. Conversations were overlapping softly around the space and the arrangement was a hit.

"Can we go over tomorrow's plan one more time," Tal asked from the other side of the table.

Maisy tuned back into the conversation, resting her elbows on the table and leaning forward. "Is there an actual plan?" she asked. "It seems like we're pretty much winging it."

Tal shrugged. "Yeah, you have a point." He frowned, tapping the surface of the table. "I hate that."

Maisy chuckled. "We all do, don't worry." She rested her chin on her hands. "There's no way around it, though. We've been all through the documentation."

"I'll start disconnecting systems in reverse order," Kit outlined. "And I just need you all to monitor." They hesitated for a moment. "Both me and the ship."

Lori cocked her head. "What problems do you expect to encounter?" she asked. "Like, can you give us an example of the kind of things that might go wrong? What should we look for?"

"We're on conversational duty again, right?" Sue asked.

"Yes, Sue. You and Joanie should continuously evaluate my speech patterns during the procedure to detect any changes in tone, speed, or coherence."

"You can read us more poetry?" Joanie asked.

"Absolutely," Kit answered. "And the teams on the *Kittridge* will monitor the systems as I disengage from them. There are automated backups on the ship that should kick in, maintaining life support, shielding, etc."

"Are those in place in case a Hitchhiker malfunctions?" Sue asked.

"Or dies," Tal added.

Kit hesitated for a moment. "Yes," they said finally. "It is the same thing, really."

"Has that happened often," Lori asked, "Hitchhikers dying on ships?"

"No," Kit said quickly. "It is very, very rare."

"How many Hitchhikers have been installed into ships?" Maisy asked, frowning.

"38."

"And how many have died?"

"Leaving their ships unmanned?" Kit asked. When Maisy nodded, they said, "Four."

Kit anticipated Maisy's next question. "One died of electrocution due to technical issues with their core. One died of asphyxiation when their oxygen line was damaged and one developed encephalitis due to an infection introduced through one of their feeds."

Maisy waited for Kit to continue, but the silence stretched on. Finally she asked, "And the fourth?"

"That termination was labeled as voluntary."

"Voluntary?" Maisy asked. She shared a glance at Sue, who nodded and began ushering Joanie from the table.

Once the little girl was out of earshot, she continued. "You're saying a Hitchhiker committed suicide," she stated bluntly.

"That is the ruling of the report," Kit answered. "And evidence seems to support that conclusion, despite the lack of any clear communications signifying intent."

"So no note," Lori clarified.

"Correct. But evaluation of recordings and logs revealed clinical signs of depression and the subject was generally unhappy with the conditions of the program."

"Did you know them?" Lori asked, her voice soft.

"I did," Kit replied, equally softly. "Her name was Mar...and she remembered."

"Remembered?" Maisy asked, frowning.

There was a silent pause before Kit responded.

"She remembered who she was."

14

Hitchhiker

The deck of the *Kittridge* lurched and Maisy held onto her console as Paulie lost his footing and tumbled onto the deck. His muffled curse sounded across the comms as the ship righted itself.

Climbing awkwardly to his feet in his vacuum suit, Paulie snarked at his brother. "Lucas, stop screwing around."

"I'm trying! I'm trying!" Entering in a final command, Lucas frowned at his brother. "I have to wait to see where the problems are before I can fix them, you know."

"You're doing great," Maisy told him without looking up from her own console. "Kit, how are you doing?"

"I'm good, Maisy," came the reply through her suit's comm. Tackling communications had been their first test that morning and now one of the *Oro*'s comm units was attached to Kit's feeds. Once they finished disengaging Kit from the ship, that would be their only means of communication.

"How is your battery holding up?" Maisy asked. That was one of the few readings they couldn't access from outside of the core.

"At current activity levels, I have three days of power available."

"Excellent," Maisy muttered, scrolling through the data. "We'll have you settled into the shuttle way before then." Tapping on the master list, Maisy took a deep breath. "Okay, guys. Everyone ready for the next set of inputs?"

After a chorus of affirmatives, Maisy cautioned, "We may lose environmentals in this segment. Make sure you have your helmets at hand if you need to suit up."

"Sever conduit B-4 when you're ready, Tal," Kit instructed. A moment later the lights flickered, but steadied.

"Maisy, can you check the oxygen levels on your panel?" Paulie asked. "They aren't showing up here."

Scrolling through the screens at her station, Maisy scanned for the reading but couldn't find it. "I don't have it here. Can I take a look?" Moving up beside Paulie, Maisy flipped through the views available on the console. "It should be on this screen."

"Kit, we don't have the atmo readings on the environmentals console on the bridge," Maisy gasped. She reached for the console as the bridge spun, her eyes tracking Paulie's slow slide to the deck.

"Helmets!" Tal was shouting over the comm, but the sound was far away and muffled.

Dropping to her knees, Maisy rolled Paulie onto his side, pushing on this helmet to release it from the bracket on his back. She slid it roughly over his head, scraping the edge along the top of his ear as her vision blackened.

The helmet clicked into place and she slumped to the floor.

***

Maisy tried to rub at the pain shooting through her head, but her hand slapped against a barrier. It took several long moments for her brain to process the sight of her hand flat against the dome of her helmet.

Squinting against the bright lights, she pushed herself upright and froze, waiting for the world to stop spinning. Across the bridge, two suited figures struggled and she moved to her knees, crawling her way toward them.

"Come on, Lucas."

Sounds filtered back into Maisy's consciousness and she recognized the strain in Paulie's voice. Wobbly on her knees, it took long seconds for her to make it to the brothers, but her head was beginning to clear.

Oxygen deprivation.

"Lucas?" Paulie was kneeling over his brother, gloved hands against the glass of his helmet.

"On?" Maisy mumbled. "Is it on?" She reached across Lucas's body to grab his arm, twisting it to see the suit's panel. The indicators were all green.

Falling back to sit on the deck, Maisy cradled her own helmet in her hands as she fought against the piercing pain behind her eyes.

"Oh, thank god," Paulie muttered.

The other sounds in Maisy's feed snapped back into focus. There were multiple voices calling her name and she tried to pick through them.

"Lori?" Maisy pushed against the deck, struggling to her feet at the desperation in Lori's voice. "Where are you?" Maisy gasped, falling back onto the deck again. Starting over, she worked her way back up to her hands and knees. There were other voices yelling for her, but she couldn't bring them into focus.

Firm hands grasped her shoulders and pulled her to her feet. Maisy kept her eyes closed, until the spinning sensation passed, then opened them cautiously. Lori's green eyes were wide and wild as they searched Maisy's.

"Oh my god, never do that again," Lori said, her gloved hands pressed against Maisy's helmet. Tears ran down her face and Maisy patted the front of her suit, searching for the console.

Finally Maisy grasped Lori's arm, checking her vitals. "You're okay," she sighed.

"Yeah," Lori held her hand over Maisy's on her arm. "We all are."

Leaning their helmets together, they stood still for a moment as Maisy took long, deep breaths.

"I'm okay," she said finally, lifting her head to look around the room. Tal and Paulie were helping Lucas, who was still a bit wobbly on his feet. Berta was standing at the environmental console.

"Was this a defense countermeasure?" Berta was asking.

"I believe it was a malfunction," Kit answered her. "If it was a countermeasure it is not documented anywhere in my database."

"Hmm." Berta didn't sound convinced, but let it drop. "Let's reroute the sensors from the secondary system into this panel." She tapped out a series of commands and moved to the next panel. "Bill, does this look good on your end?"

"All green here," came the immediate reply.

Berta took in the occupants of the bridge. "We're done for the day. Everyone head back."

****

Sue shone a light into Maisy's eyes, muttering under her breath as Joanie stood beside her, holding the instrument tray. The little girl's face was solemn as her mother returned the light and picked up a small sensor wand. On the other side of the medical bay, Helen was standing over Lucas with a similar torture device.

"I'm okay," Maisy repeated for the thousandth time, squeezing Lori's hand as she sat beside her in the medical bay. Lori's eyes were dry but her nose was still red and she clung onto Maisy's hand with a death grip

Ignoring Maisy's assurances, Sue held the wand to her neck until it pinged. Examining the results, she let out the breath she'd been holding and her posture relaxed.

"Your oxygenation levels are back to normal," she confirmed. "You all got off very lucky. Please don't do that again."

Sue set the sensor wand back on Joanie's tray and put her hands on her hips. "What's rule number one, Maisy?"

Pressing her lips together, Maisy slumped her shoulders and shrugged.

"Always put your helmet on first," Sue told her firmly. "You should know this, Maze." Sue lifted her arms in exasperation. "You can't help anyone if you asphyxiate!"

She hung her head. "I know. I'm sorry." Tears glistened in Sue's eyes a moment before Maisy was swallowed in a hug. Lori and Joanie joined in and Maisy choked back her own tears.

"I'm sorry," Maisy said again, patting Sue's shoulder awkwardly as her eyes flitted around the room. "Everyone else is okay?"

Sue pulled back and tucked Maisy's curly hair behind her ear. "They're fine. Helen is checking out the boys, but everyone looks good." She frowned again. "We can't afford to lose anyone, Maisy. You need to be more careful. If Paulie wouldn't have come around so quickly, you could have been in real trouble. You and Lucas."

"I know," Maisy said again, standing and gently moving past Sue. "Where's Tal? Berta?"

Lori stood close by her shoulder. "They went back to the *Kittridge* to try to figure out what happened. Tal's afraid there are security protocols built into the systems outside of Kit's network."

"Security protocols? This wasn't an accident?"

Lori shook her head. "It seems unlikely. The environmentals displaced all of the oxygen in seconds."

"Oh, wow," Maisy raised her hand to her head and Lori wrapped an arm around her shoulder while Joanie held onto her waist. "Well, that makes things a little more complicated, doesn't it?"

"Maisy?" A tentative voice came over the comms.

"Are you okay, Kit? What's going on?"

"Tal and Berta are heading back to the *Oro* and would like everyone to meet in the cafeteria for a debriefing," Kit said softly. "Are you well enough to attend?"

Maisy gave Lori's hand a squeeze. "I'm fine, I swear. I'll head to the cafeteria. Thanks, Kit."

"I'll go with you," Lori insisted.

Maisy caught the look Lori exchanged with Sue and swallowed her objections.

Once Sue had swept Joanie away, Maisy left the medical suite with Lori, taking it slowly. Each step was an effort, as if her shoes were pulling through mud, and she moved her head carefully. Stepping onto the elevator, Maisy swayed and Lori was right there, wrapping an arm around her waist.

"I'm fine," Maisy insisted.

Lori snorted and Maisy shrugged.

"I'm a solid 87%," she clarified, letting herself lean into Lori for a moment, their heads close together.

The doors to the elevator opened and Tal was waiting, his face tight. He took in the two of them standing close and his expression relaxed into a lopsided smile.

"Feeling better?" he asked, reaching out to take Maisy's hand as they stepped into the hallway.

"She claims to be 87%, but I feel like it's 62% at best," Lori answered with a smile.

Maisy frowned at them. "I'm feeling better by the minute. I'll be good enough to start breaking heads very shortly."

"I'll consider myself warned," Tal replied solemnly as they walked into the cafeteria.

"You guys sit down and I'll grab coffee." Tal veered toward the food processors as Maisy maneuvered herself carefully into the crowded bench beside Jane, trying to give the impression that her head wasn't pounding.

Across from her, Berta sat with a frown on her face, her gaze focused into the distance. A moment later Tal returned with a tray of cups for the table and sat down beside Berta. Lori snagged two cups for herself and Maisy as Berta began.

"Kit, what can you tell us about the security protocols on the *Kittridge*?" she asked.

"I've been trying to access them since the incident and they're behind a firewall that I can't breach." There was a faint undertone of frustration behind Kit's usual calm voice.

Berta sighed. "I suspected as much. Tal and I have been discussing the possibility that this is by design." She nodded toward Tal and he picked up the line of conversation.

"We think the incident this morning may be part of a set of SN protocols to deal with Kit being compromised by an outside force."

"Like pirates?" Lori asked.

"Like the missiles on the *Sky*." Maisy added, realization dawning. "They were protecting themselves against corporate espionage."

"Basically," Tal agreed. "It seems likely that they had a backup plan in case Kit needed to be...lobotomized."

The blood left Maisy's face and Lori gasped beside her as Kit said firmly, "Chief engineer Snow wouldn't have allowed something like that."

Tal shrugged, "She may not have known."

"Or maybe she did and that's why she had such a bad relationship with Captain Twig," Berta suggested. "We've seen her log posts, and you said they fought."

There was a moment of silence, then Kit began speaking in a distracted voice, "I'm going back through my recordings." After another pause, they said, "There is evidence to support your theory."

A video projection rose along the long axis of the table. It was a hallway in the *Kittridge*. A door opened and two figures stepped out, mid conversation.

"This is outside of the Captain's quarters," Kit noted. "The one place on the *Kittridge* that I could not access."

Captain Twig was a slight man, with a sneer on his face as he said, "It's just a failsafe, Snow. Get over it."

"It is indicative of a lack of respect for sentient life that I find abhorrent," Chief Snow replied in a cool, calm tone. She was a compact woman with a square jaw, her hair matching her name.

"I don't want to have this conversation out here," Twig replied, turning away from her and walking down the hallway.

Snow fell into step beside him, catching up without seeming to hurry. "Would you not agree that a person without legs is still a person?"

Twig cut his eyes toward her. "I'm warning you, Snow. You know damn well that thing isn't a person."

"If you lost your arms, would you not still expect to be treated as a sentient being?"

Twig ignored her, walking faster.

The Chief took a long stride and cut in front of Twig, forcing him to stop. "You can't just turn them off like a switch." She crossed her arms over her chest and stared the Captain down.

Twig pushed past her, his elbow hitting her chest. "Do your job and I won't have to."

The recording stayed with Snow, showing the frown on her face and her clenched fists as Twig disappeared off screen.

"So," Maisy thought out loud, "we've already probably disabled some of these kill switches by rerouting the bio support lines, right?"

There were nods around the table.

"Then the good news is that most of the remaining attacks are probably aimed at repelling boarders, like the oxygen deprivation."

Jane shook her head, "Not necessarily. I've been going through the documentation Kit has sent us on the Hitchhiker Program and I think we're underestimating how integrated the ship's network is into Kit's neural net."

"Can't Kit just cut the feeds?" Lori asked.

"It would be like asking you to cut off feeling to your arm. It's a part of you. Not only can you not voluntarily cut it out of your awareness, but if it was suddenly removed by force it would be traumatic enough to send you into shock."

Maisy leaned forward. "You're saying that by removing Kit from the ship, we may throw them into shock?"

Jane gestured at the tablet sitting before her on the table. "Not if we do it the right way."

"What's the right way?" Maisy asked. "Now that Kit is running on tanks, the clock is ticking."

"I project that we have 48 hours before my tanks would need to be refilled or replaced," Kit added.

"That should give us plenty of time," Jane said. "According to Chief Snow's documentation, every system of the *Kittridge* has a separate neural pathway into Kit's core. If we shut them down one by one and link them up to the corresponding systems on the shuttle, we should be able to mitigate the trauma of the move."

"Can we do that remotely?" Lori asked.

"I believe I will be able to connect to the shuttle while still being physically on the *Kittridge*," Kit confirmed.

Tal sighed. "So all we have to do is rewire your brain from one body to new one while your old body tries to kill us?"

"Exactly."

15

The Saboteur

Maisy sat at the table watching Tal and Jane standing before the huge diagram stretching across two walls and tried not to cross her eyes. The drawing was so detailed that there were circuits she couldn't see from a foot away. She knew because she'd tried. At this point, she'd given up.

"Where is the relay circuit for the temperature sensor on the forward positioning thrusters? We've lost that somewhere." Jane was squinting at her segment of the diagram, stress in her voice.

"Wait," Tal said, running over to her side. "Wait, wait...here it is." He tapped an area of the wall and a red dot highlighted the circuit. "We had to combine it with the one on this side because the shuttle only has one, remember?"

Jane held a hand to her head. "That's right!"

"Guys, let's take a break and have Kit review the plan," Maisy suggested. They'd been at it for nearly twelve hours straight and her head was spinning.

"I'm testing all of the circuits and comparing them to the diagram now," Kit reported. "I expect the test to take 4.7 minutes."

"I need more coffee," Tal muttered, dropping into a seat at the table.

Maisy pushed herself up to her feet. "I'll get it. You guys sit." Her headache was finally gone and it was good to get up and move.

In the cafeteria there were a few passengers scattered across the long tables. At one end Bill sat alone, his plate empty before him. As Maisy approached the processors, Bill got up with his tray and brought it to the recycler.

"Hi, Maisy," he said with a slight frown. "I'm glad to see you're feeling better."

She forced a smile. "Thanks, Bill. It really wasn't that big of a deal."

Bill's frown grew deeper. "We can't afford to lose you, Maisy."

Taken aback, Maisy dropped her fake smile and echoed the pilot's frown. "We can't afford to lose anyone."

"You were right before," Bill started. "That not everyone is pulling their weight–"

Maisy interrupted him. "That doesn't matter. We need everyone."

"Do we?" Bill shook his head. "I still think you're doing too much, but the fact of the matter is that we need you to do it." His face softened a little. "We need you, Maisy. And I'm grateful that you're on board."

With that the older man set his tray in the recycler and walked away, leaving Maisy staring after him with a furrowed brow.

"Weird," she muttered under her breath. Sighing, she shook off the encounter and gathered three cups of coffee to take back to the meeting room.

The conversation was still replaying in her head as she set the cups on the table and Tal reached out to touch her hand.

"Everything okay?," he asked, taking one of the cups.

Jane leaned across the desk and grabbed one as well, then jumped to her feet to begin pacing before the diagram again.

"Did Kit find any issues?" Maisy asked Tal, her eyes on Jane's harried form.

"A couple," Tal said, rubbing his eyes. "But we've resolved them. I think we're ready to start moving these inputs."

Maisy opened her mouth to object but Tal held up a hand.

"In the morning," he agreed. "We're all beat."

***

Maisy returned to her suite after midnight ship's time and found the main living area dark. Padding through by the soft glow of the safety lights, she entered the bedroom she shared with Lori.

She slipped off her shoes and sat on the side of the bed for a moment in the darkness, her mind empty.

"Maisy," Kit's voice whispered in her ear.

She whipped her head around to gaze at Lori's sleeping form and got up quickly from the bed and moved into the bathroom. As she closed the door the lights brightened and her pale reflection appeared over the sink.

"What's up?" she answered softly.

"Loy has left his room and is on his way to the shuttle bay," Kit answered.

Maisy threw her hands up, slamming out of the bathroom. "You should have led with that." Sliding her feet into her shoes, Maisy leaned over to shake Lori's shoulder.

Lori sat up, rubbing her eyes. "What's going on?"

"Loy is heading back to the shuttle bay," Maisy told her grimly and walked quickly out the door.

"Wait!" Lori yelled, flinging off the blanket and scrambling for her shoes. "Kit, have Tal meet her there!"

Lori caught up with Maisy before the elevator doors closed, sliding in to stand at her shoulder.

"Tal is on his way," Kit announced as they stepped out, "but Loy has passed the shuttle and is heading toward the secondary maintenance bay."

Maisy's brow furrowed and she glanced at Lori, "Now what?"

Kit's voice sounded above them with urgency. "Maisy, hurry."

Breaking into a run, Maisy asked, "What is he doing? Is he damaging the suits we stored in there?"

"I don't think he's interested in the suits. Hurry, Maisy."

Oh, crap. Maisy put on a burst of speed, Lori on her heels. "Kit, can you lock the hatch?"

"I don't have access to the controls. I tried talking to him, but he's ignoring me."

"Crap," she gasped, running flat out.

Tal's tall form appeared from the other end of the hallway, his long legs closing the distance. "Stay back," he yelled, swinging into the secondary maintenance bay.

The hatch slid shut behind him and Maisy slammed into it. Slapping the pad, she banged a fist against the door. "Open the hatch!"

Maisy hit the comms button on the panel. "Bridge! Who's on the bridge?"

Coming to a stop beside her, Lori bent over at the waist, gasping. "Kit, who's on the bridge? Have them open the hatch from there."

Maisy banged on the hatch again. "Tal!" She flinched back as the door opened and lurched forward to slide through the gap.

Inside the small maintenance bay the lights were still dim and Maisy swept the room once before her eyes picked out Tal's slumped form before the airlock.

The rest of the bay was empty.

"Maisy! What's going on down there? Gary said..." Berta's voice trailed away, uncharacteristically tentative.

Maisy walked to Tal's side and hit the button to close the outer airlock door. The space beyond was empty.

"Maisy?" Berta asked again.

"Loy is gone," Maisy told her softly. She wrapped her arms around Tal's waist. Lori joined them and they both held him while his body shook.

***

With the exception of Bill, who was manning the bridge, all of the remaining fifty-one passengers of the *Oro* sat in the cafeteria. No one made eye contact and the silence was deafening.

Finally Berta rose, clearing her throat. After looking down at the table top for a moment longer, she lifted her head and surveyed the room.

"I don't really know you," she said into the silence. "None of us chose to be here and like many of you, I've been sulking. I've been spending a lot of my time alone in my room when I should have been out here."

Berta met each gaze as she spoke, her eyes moving from one passenger to the next. "I didn't know Loy."

The room took a collective breath at his name. Gazes dropped to table tops as Berta continued. "When he destroyed the support systems we were setting up for Kit in the shuttle, I was mad. I was angry and frustrated. I wondered what was wrong with him, but I didn't actually ask."

Berta pressed her lips together and nodded to herself, tilting her head. "I just assumed he was a bigot," she shrugged.

There was a rumble of sound around the room. And her eyes snapped up to scan for the source.

"Did *anyone* here know Loy?" she asked the room at large.

Silence. Maisy glanced around their table. No one spoke up.

"Did anyone talk to him? Who did he sit with for meals?"

A few tentative hands raised.

Helen spoke softly, "I've sat across from him, but we only said hi, really." She grimaced, frowning. "Sean knew him better, I think. They played games together over the network."

But Sean had bailed and chosen the cryobay, was left unsaid.

Curtis spoke up, from the furthest table. "He had a kid."

An inhale swept the room.

"On the station. I think. I saw him with a kid," Curtis shrugged, looking like he was in pain.

Berta swept the room again. "No one else knew him? From before?"

Heads shook in response but no one else spoke up. Berta singled out a man at the next table. "Sander? You shared a room with him?"

"A bathroom," he corrected quickly. "We each had our own bedroom." He pressed his lips together. "I didn't know him. I didn't try. We've all had so much to deal with and I've just been spending most of my time in my room, watching vids."

There were nods around the room.

"That's what a lot of us have been doing," said the woman seated across from Helen. She reached out and patted Helen's casted arm and she smiled back wanly.

Berta looked around, spotting the tablet sitting on the table in front of Jane. "What did he say when we were collecting names in the beginning?"

Jane picked up the tab and opened the passenger list they had created during those first few hectic days aboard the *Oro*. She scrolled, looking for his entry. "Loy Gerald," she read. "Ore processing machinist, level 2." Jane looked up. "That's it. There's nothing else."

Berta sighed, leaning a hip against the end of the table, arms folded across her chest. "We have to do better."

She glanced down and swept the people at the first table with her gaze. Tal, Maisy, Jane, Sue, Lori. When her gaze touched Joanie, Berta's expression softened.

"We're all in this together. We have to watch out for each other, pay attention to each other." She looked up and down the long tables. "We're a family now, like it or not, and we only have each other to depend on."

There were nods at her words.

"We failed Loy," she declared bluntly. "We have to do better."

***

Everyone deserved a day of rest, but the clock was ticking. They needed to get Kit's inputs transferred over to the shuttle before they could cut the core out of the *Kittridge* and time was running out. They could refill the tanks indefinitely and recharge the battery, but leaving Kit attached to the temporary supply lines on an unstable ship was dangerous in and of itself. The faster the transfer was accomplished, the better.

Maisy and Tal were fully suited on the bridge of the *Kittridge*, while the rest of the team worked from the shuttle on board the *Oro*. For safety's sake, they'd decided to minimize the number of people on the *Kittridge*. No one was taking safety lightly this time.

Kit had been able to get them access to the engineering panels and they worked in silence as they manually changed over circuit after circuit.

"Can you ping number four, Kit?" Maisy asked softly.

"Looks good," came the immediate answer. "Are you seeing that, Paulie?"

"Yup, loud and clear," Paulie responded over the comm to the *Oro*. "Checking the auxiliaries system off the list, guys."

Maisy sighed. "We're almost there."

Beside her Tal compared the readout on his tablet with the data scrolling past on the panel. "We're ready to reroute thrusters."

"Once I disconnect from the ship's thrusters, we may lose the skybridge," Kit warned. "I won't be able to counter any drift caused by debris or the torquing of the ship as the crack widens."

"Understood," Tal replied. "If the tunnel fails we'll jet back to the *Oro*."

Maisy frowned. "That won't damage the *Oro*, will it?"

"No, the structure is designed to tear at junctions if there's too much pressure. It will collapse before it can damage either ship," Kit assured her.

She nodded, pushing aside her concern with a sigh. "Okay, then. Let's finish this."

***

The last indicator switched to red and, just like that, Kit was cut off from the ship that had been their body for their entire life. The rudimentary backup systems engaged and Maisy rolled her shoulders to release the tension there.

"I think that's it," she said, stepping back from the console.

"That was the last one," Kit agreed. "I can't see the *Kittridge*'s systems at all. It's completely dark."

Tal frowned. "But you can see the shuttle, right?"

"A little. I can't really feel it yet."

Tal and Maisy shared a look.

"It will get better," Kit assured them. "I'll integrate into its system in time."

"And you can hear and see us?" Maisy let the question trail off, since she knew the answer.

"It's like a transplant," Kit said. "It isn't instantaneous. But it's better than nothing and I'm very happy to be here."

"We're very happy to have you," Maisy replied.

16

Project Melon Baller

"I think you're overestimating my abilities," Tal said as he slowly rotated against the backdrop of a million stars. Above him the white skybridge extended between the two ships like a plastisteel umbilical cord. He contemplated the large circle etched onto the starboard hull of the *Kittridge*, then turned his frown to the two meter long laser floating before him.

He tried again. "Suddenly this seems like a really bad idea." Tal spun slowly to face Maisy and Berta.

"You've got this," Maisy told him. "Just fire the laser along that line."

"This isn't a melon baller," Tal objected. "It's more like Project Swiss Cheese."

"Apple corer?" Maisy offered.

"This was literally your idea," Berta pointed out.

"Yeah," Tal agreed, "but I didn't think I'd have to be the one to do it."

"You're the one with the most experience operating the laser," Maisy reminded him.

"From a console!" Tal used his thrusters to spin back to face the laser. It was as long as he was, and twice as wide. "I've never removed one from the ship's mount and shot it like a frackin' rifle before."

Maisy attempted to shrug in her vacuum suite. "Consider it a learning experience, kid."

Tal froze at the familiar phrase, letting himself spin back toward her. "Your dad used to say that." He angled his head towards Maisy and met her gaze. "I wish he was here."

"Yeah, me too."

Berta's sigh was loud over the comm. "There's no point in delaying this any longer, Tal. Let's start making these cuts," she said firmly. "Are you ready, Kit?"

"I am. The ship has been completely depressurized. You may proceed."

"Slow and steady," Berta said.

"Yeah," Tal sighed. "Slow and steady. Right."

Bracing his shoulders, Tal wrapped his arms around the body of the laser and manhandled it into place. He aimed past the edge of the *Kittridge* and engaged the makeshift switch he'd constructed on the side of the large barrel. There was very little recoil, but he drifted backwards gently, his tether to Maisy rippling.

Tal swept the long barrel upward and the beam made contact with the ship and a furrow appeared in the outer hull of the *Kittridge*, its edges glowing orange. The invisible line continued its path into the ship and the groove deepened, leaving behind a molten edge of glowing orange rivulets that flowed and then darkened as they hardened. The entire process took less than a second. The laser superheated the metals of the ship and the cold vacuum of space cooled it again, making it seem that the beam ate through the material.

Moving slowly, Tal inched toward the line they'd drawn on the hull. They'd spent hours examining 3D models and scans to figure out the safe zone around Kit's core, but they were all tense.

"Kit, check in, please," Maisy asked. "Can you confirm that the line is where we thought it would be?"

"We're within the tolerance, Maisy."

She nodded inside the dome of her helmet. "Let us know if it gets close to the limit. Sue, you guys good there?"

"We're good, Maze. Kit is reading poetry," Sue responded immediately. She and Joanie were again tasked with engaging Kit in conversation to detect any mental changes. "Joanie asked for Emily Dickinson. She said it was your favorite."

"It is," Maisy confirmed with a sad smile.

"Joanie described the poem you'd read to her and I found it for her," Kit added. "I had not heard of this poet before. I find her intriguing."

"She was my mother's favorite." Maisy sighed. "I brought a book of her poems with me from Earth, but I lost it on the Citadel."

"I often wonder about my parents," Kit said softly. "What they were like."

The glow of the laser's beam had reached the outline of the circle on Kit's hull and Tal began following its curve.

"You don't know anything about them?" Maisy asked, her tone echoing Kit's.

"There is little information in the records I have access to," Kit said. "But it appears that they were killed before I was commissioned."

"Killed?" Maisy took her eyes off the laser's path and tilted her head. "By SN? Were they part of the Hitchhiker project too?"

"In a way," Kit answered. "Tal, we are outside of the tolerance."

Tal immediately cut the stream, swearing.

***

Through trial and error they recalibrated and expanded the target zone for Tal's laser.

"Think of it from the opposite angle," Maisy told Tal as he realigned his makeshift tool. "Rather than scooping out Kit's core, think of it as cutting away enough of the ship to reveal the core." She waved a gloved hand at the expanse of shielded metal plating before them. "If you can just cut away a small enough chunk that includes Kit, we can bring the core into the shuttle bay and keep working on it there." Maisy shrugged beneath the stiff shoulders of her vacuum suit. "At least it would be a lot easier without the suits."

Tal nodded, but didn't respond, his gaze intense as he maneuvered the laser back into position. "Ok, I'm ready to start again. You ready, Kit?"

"I'm ready, Tal."

"Okay," Tal said again, blowing out a long breath. "We've got this."

The laser once again began eating a line through the hull of the *Kittridge*. From ten thousand meters away, during a dogfight, a laser might sear through layers of plating to hit pressurized living spaces, igniting oxygen. Close enough it might melt through decks, destroying multiple compartments further into the interior of a ship. But at this distance, the laser was a scalpel, cutting away the damaged part of Kit's body so that the crew of the *Oro* could implant their core into a new host.

Tal cut away at sections of the *Kittridge* for hours. Layer after layer, panel after panel the interior of the ship was revealed, like layers of an onion. As he came to the end of the current cut, he blinked sweat from his eyes and opened a large section of the *Kittridge* to space. Letting his shoulders sag, he hung before it, spinning slowly.

Working together, Maisy and Berta removed the newly freed section of the ship and pushed it gently away from the *Oro*. The large pieces of metal and plastisteel Tal had already cut away hung in a slow motion blast radius around the *Kittridge*.

"We are 67% completed with this task," Kit announced.

Tal grimaced under the dome of his helmet. "I have to take a break, guys. My hands are starting to shake."

"I've been watching you, I think I can take a turn," Maisy offered. She pulled herself along the tether to close the distance between them and gingerly accepted the awkward shape of the laser barrel as Tal handed it off.

He shook out his arms, then demonstrated the controls.

"It's basically just point and shoot," Maisy observed wryly.

"True," Tal muttered, watching Maisy wrestle with the long, wide body of the laser.

"Stupid inertia," she grumbled. "This is harder than it looks."

Berta moved up beside her and the two of them got the laser into place before Berta let herself drift back again. Tal stayed at Maisy's side as she prepared to engage the beam.

"Starting now, Kit," Maisy called over the comm.

"I'm ready, Maisy."

"Lucas, all green in the shuttle?" Berta asked.

"All good in here," came the immediate response.

"Everything sounds good in there too," Sue offered.

Berta nodded at Maisy. "Okay, let's go."

Maisy depressed the switch and the target area on the *Kittridge* began to heat and melt. She pushed gently against the wide body of the laser housing and the line moved slowly across the surface.

The plating was relatively easy to cut through. Bulkheads took the longest. An hour later, Maisy grunted as she repositioned the laser to attack the last bulkhead between them and Kit's core. She'd already cut one end. When she finished the cut on the other side, she let out a little cheer.

"Good job," Berta said briskly. "Let's get this out of here."

Maisy stood back with the laser as Berta and Tal tugged the long block of reinforced tungsten out of the way and pushed it away from the ship. It glided away and revealed the smooth, curved surface beneath.

"Kit?" Maisy whispered. "Is that you?"

"It is part of me," they answered. "The part you're saving."

Maisy frowned. "I'm sorry we couldn't save the ship."

"The engines were gone," Kit pointed out pragmatically. "There was nothing left to repair. The shuttle is small, but versatile. I'll be able to fly to the surface, which is not something the *Kittridge* was designed for."

"We will have adventures," Maisy promised.

"I'm looking forward to it, Maisy."

***

By the time they'd freed Kit's core, Maisy was drenched in sweat. Her curls stuck uncomfortably to her forehead under her helmet's dome and she was generally sore, tired, and miserable.

"It's time for a break," Berta announced.

Maisy groaned. "We're so close."

"Maneuvering Kit's core into the shuttle bay isn't going to be easy. And we'll need more hands," Berta pointed out. "Let's all rest and then we'll start fresh.

"How much time do we have, Kit?" Maisy asked.

"I have over 14 hours on the tanks, Maisy. Plenty of time for you to rest."

"Okay," Maisy sighed.

The three of them used their thrusters to return to the *Oro* and tethered the laser to the hull before entering the airlock. Maisy lurched as the ship's gravity snagged her tired body, but stayed upright. Beside her, Tal wavered as they stepped through the hatch.

Removing her helmet, Maisy gave a sigh of relief as she could finally push her damp curls off of her forehead and rub at her tired eyes.

Berta gave her a small smile as she efficiently removed her suit and set it back perfectly into its locker. It took Maisy much longer to struggle out of hers, but eventually the three of them were walking down to the cafeteria.

Smiling faces greeted them.

"You're almost done," Joanie clapped her hands. "Kit showed us a hologram of what you were doing. It was so cool!"

"It was so hard!" Maisy corrected her, laughing tiredly. "Let's get some dinner and then I'm going to pass out."

As they returned from the dispenser with their plates, Lori bumped Maisy's shoulder gently. "We were watching on the shuttle, too," she said. "Joanie's right, it looked pretty cool." She smiled widely. "That laser is literally bigger than you are."

"Yeah," Maisy agreed tiredly. "It's like wrestling a tree trunk."

Lori raised her eyebrows, "Well, it looks very impressive."

Maisy chuckled weakly as she slid into the table. "Thanks." She took a bite of her shrimp and rice and sighed. "I'm hoping the really hard part is done."

"It is, Maisy," Kit chimed in. "You've done an amazing job." Kit paused and continued in a more formal tone. "You all have, and I just wanted to say thank you. Without your help, I would have died out here. Alone. Thank you for allowing me to join you on the *Oro*."

"We're very happy to have you join us, Kit," Maisy said softly, her voice thick.

Tal cleared his throat. "Without your help, the journey to 761 would have taken us almost a year—if we made it at all. The supplies and expertise you've leant us has made a huge difference to this entire crew and we are really lucky to have you."

Maisy nodded, holding back tears. Lori squeezed her hand, her own eyes glistening.

"Welcome to the family, Kit," Joanie said with a smile.

17

Moving Day

"I would like to not have to wear this suit again for a few days," Maisy grumbled as she inserted her legs into the stiff pants. "Also, we need to add checking the sanitizer to the list because I can still smell myself from yesterday."

"Are you sure it's coming from the suit and not you?" Lori joked, bursting into a laugh when Maisy shot her a crude gesture.

Tal stuck his head into the suit he was holding up and sniffed loudly. "Mine smells fine. Must just be you, Maze."

"You guys are a riot." Maisy stood up and began pulling the upper body of the suit over her shoulders. "I'll remember this."

On the other side of the maintenance bay, Paulie and Lucas were helping each other adjust their suits. Berta stood behind Curtis, attaching his helmet, her own suit already sealed.

"I'm ready," Maisy announced as she closed the last latch at the neck of her suit.

Lori picked up the helmet sitting beside her on the bench and handed it to Maisy. "Don't forget this," she smiled.

"No." Maisy's smile fell away and she looked toward the airlock hatch. "I won't."

Lori followed her gaze and her eyes widened with realization. "I didn't..."

"No, I know," Maisy shook her head, squeezing her gloved hand awkwardly. Shaking off the memories, Maisy attached her helmet, listening for the hiss that indicated a good seal.

The sound echoed several times around the room as everyone finished suiting up. Maisy surveyed the gathered volunteers and smiled.

"I think we're ready, Kit. We're coming to get you."

"I'm here," Kit replied.

They exited through the airlock in two cycles, Tal leading the first with Lucas and Paulie with the pallet of thrusters and Berta leading the second with Curtis and Maisy. As they waited for Tal's group to clear the exterior hatch, Maisy double checked everyone's tethers on the second team. She was the last one out of the door and as soon as they'd cycled through the outer hatch, she latched the end of the tether to the exterior hook on the *Oro*'s hull.

"We're all hooked up," she said over the comm and Tal gave her a thumb's up from where he floated.

Together the six of them moved slowly to the *Kittridge* with the pallet of thrusters, Tal in the lead and Maisy bringing up the rear.

"Everyone be careful," Tal's voice came over the comm. "Kit's core is super heavy and it's going to be unwieldy. But we only have to get it from here to the *Oro*. Slow and steady, right?"

Choruses of agreement echoed over the line as they finally came up to the *Kittridge*'s hull. The area around the exposed egg of the core looked like it had been chewed on by rats or impacted by a very small meteor shower. The impact site was several meters deep into the side of the ship and revealed crudely cut walls and beams with scalloped edges. The core itself was still attached to sections of wall holding the temporary support tanks the crew from the *Oro* had tacked into place, but otherwise it was floating freely at the center of the *Kittridge*'s wound.

Maisy had cut away enough material around the core to allow a suited person to move freely and Tal maneuvered himself into that space, navigating around the sharp edges carefully.

"Okay, guys," he said. "Just like we went over before, these are low charge thrusters and they should have just enough force to give us about one meter per second of acceleration. There are magnets on the back so they just slap onto any flat surface. Let's start with one in the back and see if we can get Kit out of this hole."

Lucas passed the first disc-shaped thruster to Tal and he slapped it against the side of Kit's core like an old-fashioned landmine. Adjusting the position slightly, Tal moved back out of the hole and stood a safe distance away as he prepared to fire the thruster from the panel built into the forearm of his suit.

"Here we go, everyone. Fire in the hole!" Tal tapped the panel and light flared from behind the core, flooding the area and spilling out around the edges. The large, egg-shaped bulk began moving up and out of the hole slowly.

"Can you feel that, Kit?" Maisy asked excitedly. "The movement?"

"I can't feel it," Kit said, "but I'm watching on the *Oro*'s feeds." Kit hesitated. "I'm distracting myself with the shuttle's lights and sensors."

Joanie's bright voice cut into the line. "It's so cool, Maze! Kit is making rainbows on the inside of the shuttle bay."

"It's psychedelic," Sue muttered. "I think it's giving me a migraine."

"I'm so sorry, Sue. I'll tone it down," Kit said contritely.

"It's okay, Kit! I'm just kidding. The colors are beautiful," Sue assured them.

Maisy smiled at their antics as Kit's core emerged from the wreck of the *Kittridge*. "I'm glad you guys are having fun."

"We are," Kit said.

Tal drifted back to the core as it cleared the hole they'd cut.

"Ready for the second thruster," he said.

Lucas passed him another disc and he attached it halfway down the long side of Kit's egg.

"Okay, firing the second thruster now." A round flash of light appeared briefly on the side of the core with no discernible effect.

"Bill, can you analyze the updated trajectory? Looks like we need another ignition on that second thruster."

Bill's voice came back a second later. "Confirmed, Tal. You are seven degrees off target."

"The force of the thrusters against the hull has accelerated the spin," Kit reported calmly. "We're about to lose the skybridge."

The long curving cylinder that stretched between the two ships was twisting faster. As the torque reached its threshold, the junctions separated. Within seconds the segments were moving away from the two ships.

"Holy crap," Paulie whispered into the comm.

Kit's tone was still calm. "It's okay. We were expecting this, Paulie."

"We're still on track," Tal said as he used the thrusters in his suit to position himself on the other side of the egg. Eyeing the line toward the *Oro*, he made a minute adjustment to the position of the 2nd thruster.

"Firing again."

This time the egg's flight path angled as it inched away from the *Kittridge*.

"How is that looking, Bill?" Tal asked.

"Looking good from here, Tal." Bill came back immediately.

Tal did an awkward fist bump in his vacuum suite and the other volunteers closed on the core. "Let's check all of the connections before we increase speed."

As they swarmed over the egg, Berta called out the checklist items one by one.

"Lucas, did you check that tank brace?" she asked. "Kit, is your oxygen flow okay?"

"All of my systems are green," Kit responded.

Berta tapped her suit panel to close the checklist. "Okay, we're good to increase speed."

Tal moved into position behind the core. "Okay, that looks good. I'm ready to fire the thruster. Everyone ready?"

"Ready," Maisy called as she gripped onto part of a bulkhead still attached to the core. Beside her the others did the same and echoed her call.

"You still good in there, Kit?" Maisy said softly.

"Hi, Maisy. I'm here. I'm okay."

Maisy patted the hard surface gently. "Alright, let's bring you home."

"Firing now," Tal called and the core moved forward gently.

Ahead, the *Oro* floated against the softly spinning backdrop of the windless sky, endlessly black and full of stars. There was no sun or point of reference close enough to give their movement context. There was only the two ships and the small metal egg moving between them.

"Why does it feel like we're falling?" Paulie's question broke the silence.

Tal chuckled softly. "Don't worry. It's just your brain trying to make sense of movement in a zero gravity environment."

"Right," Paulie answered, sounding unconvinced.

"We're just going for a little stroll," Lori added, a smile in her voice.

Lucas barked out a laugh. "With a baby carriage!" They all chuckled.

Berta sighed, "More like we had to deliver the baby via cesarean."

"And Tal was the doctor!" Paulie added.

"You guys are approaching the halfway point." Bill cut through their chuckles. "I'm opening the shuttle bay doors."

"Maisy." Kit's voice echoed oddly, with a robotic reverberation in the middle. "Maisy, something's wrong."

Maisy reached out a hand to touch the surface of the core. "Is it one of the feeds?" Her eyes searched over the connections within her view. "Lucas, can you see the oxygen line?"

"There are toxins in my system," Kit said, their voice slow and distorted.

Tal called over the comm, "Sue, do you see anything on your readouts?" He used his thrusters to circle the moving core, visually examining each connection.

"I don't see any issues here," Berta called from her position.

Tal pulled up his panel and scanned the connections, looking for leaks as they all scrambled over the core, checking in.

Sue's voice cut through the chatter. "Kit's right, a toxin has been introduced to their system." She cried out. "It's poison! I don't know what to do!"

"Holy shit," Bill cried out. "Get back on the ship. Now!"

Berta's voice was low and calm by comparison. "What's going on, Bill?"

Bill babbled over the line, his words tripping over each other. "The *Kittridge* is sending out a self-destruct warning. Get back on the ship! Get back on the ship!"

Faintly, through interference and under the din of overlapping voices, Kit whispered, "Maisy, I'm sorry."

"Kit?" Maisy pressed her hands against the outside of the core. "What's going on? *Kit!*"

Sue sobbed, "He's gone. Kit is gone." and faintly in the background Joanie's voice was high and panicked. Over it all, Bill was screaming at them.

"Everyone quiet!" Berta's voice cut across the comm. "Jane, what's going on?"

"The *Kittridge* is broadcasting a self-destruct warning," Jane answered, but Bill spoke over her.

"It's going to blow," he bit out. "Get back here now!"

Maisy banged against the outside of the core, "Kit! What's your status?"

Tal was beside her, wrapping her hands in his. "We have to go, Maze."

"Get off me," she snarled. "Kit, answer me!"

"Maisy, there's no electrical activity. Kit's organic components are dead. I'm so sorry," Sue said.

"They're gone. We have to go," Tal grabbed her, pulling her from the core and Maisy wrestled away to bang against the metal shell.

Sue was sobbing faintly, repeating, "I'm sorry, I'm so sorry," over and over again and Joanie called Kit's name.

"Everyone back on the *Oro*," Berta called out and the volunteers released their grips on the egg and used their thrusters to push toward the ship.

Bill's voice was calmer. "It's started a countdown. Get back here now. I'm cycling up the engines."

"Wait for us, Bill," Berta commanded firmly.

"Then hurry!" Bill yelled, his calm gone. "We have to go!"

Jane's voice cut over his. "We'll wait, Berta," she said firmly.

Tal wrapped his arms and legs around Maisy, twisting his body to break her grip. "Lori, help me!"

"Get off me!" Maisy cried. "Kit's not dead! We're not leaving them!"

"We have to go!" Tal yelled back. "Lori, grab her legs!"

Trapped between the two of them, Maisy's gaze was locked on the core as they raced toward the *Oro*.

"No! Kit? *Kit!*"

The comm was full of panting and faint sobs.

"Tal, use the starboard thrusters to push the core into a lateral trajectory. I don't want the blast sending it into the *Oro*," Berta commanded, her voice breathy with exertion but still calm.

"Copy," Tal said shortly.

A moment later glowing discs appeared on one side of the core as Maisy's wide, dry eyes tracked its progress.

"Lori, let me go," Maisy said in a voice like gravel.

Lori shook her head inside her helmet, pressed against Maisy's waist, and held on tighter. Maisy relaxed the hand that had been pushing against Lori's shoulder and just let it rest there as they passed through the shuttle bay doors and dropped to the deck as they were caught by the ship's gravity. All around them, the others landed with various levels of success.

"Bill, we're all in," Berta called and the bay doors immediately closed. The deck beneath them thrummed with the vibrations of the engines cycling up.

"I'm maxing out the engines," Jane said from far away.

"10 seconds to detonation," Bill added.

There was no port in the shuttle bay doors. Maisy gaze burned a hole in the blank plastisteel surface, her eyes locked on the last location she'd seen Kit's core as it floated away from the *Oro*.

Paulie was struggling to his feet and Berta rapped out, "Stay down," as Jane's voice came over the comm.

"Brace for impact," she said calmly.

The deck beneath their bodies heaved and the lights went out, leaving them in absolute darkness.

18

Shockwaves

"We're okay. We made it." Jane's voice was faint in the dark.

The emergency lights flickered and came on, bathing the shuttle bay in a faint red glow. Maisy pushed herself to her knees and gloved hands pulled her to her feet. It took her eyes a moment to make sense of the monochromatic world around her.

"Lori," she recognized, finally, clinging to the hands holding her up. All around them suited figures struggled to their feet, unfamiliar shapes with their domes shadowed and flat under the pale crimson lights.

"Are you okay? Maisy, can you hear me?" Lori was saying.

Finally processing her questions, Maisy nodded. Another figure approached them and reached out to remove her helmet. She wondered briefly if there was oxygen in the bay, but didn't struggle. The helmet was lifted up and pushed back over her shoulders. She took a deep breath.

"Maisy," Tal said.

"I'm okay," she answered without thinking.

Tal released the seal on Lori's helmet and pushed it back. Maisy stared at Lori's red hair. The lights came back on but Lori's hair was still red.

Maybe I'm not okay, Maisy thought.

Without the strange red cast, the shuttle bay looked completely normal.

"Let's get back to the maintenance bay and out of these suits, everyone," Berta called across the group. She led the way down the corridor and into the maintenance bay, where they worked together to get everyone out of their suits.

Maisy's mind was comfortably blank as she hung up her suit and put away her helmet. She allowed Lori to lead her out of the bay and to the cafeteria. There Lori parked her at a table and returned a moment later with steaming cups and plates.

Maisy raised the cup to her nose, expecting coffee. "Chocolate?" She asked.

"Drink it," Lori said firmly, sitting beside her.

Sue appeared by her side, a tearful Joanie in tow. Maisy sat her mug down carefully as Sue pulled her into a hug.

"I think she's in shock," Lori said, but Maisy didn't respond. The pressure of Sue's arms around her was breaking through her shell. She leaned her head against the older woman's shoulder as tears welled up and fell.

***

Tal

Tal followed Berta into the bridge and walked immediately to the telemetry console, where Jane stood, pale and shaken.

As Berta grilled Bill on recent events, Tal pulled Jane into a hug. She let her blonde head rest on his shoulder for a moment before pulling back.

"I need to go down to the cryobay to make sure everything's okay," she said quietly.

Tal nodded. "We've got this. Go."

She squeezed his hand again and slipped away.

Tal sighed, pulling up the readings from the past hour. As the recordings from the *Kittridge* played, Berta and Bill came up to stand at his shoulder.

Warning. Restricted property of the Suki-Nyberg Corporation has been removed from this vessel. This vessel will self-destruct in one minute.

"They mean Kit?" Tal asked.

"We removed a lot of material from the *Kittridge*, but the timing would suggest it was the removal of Kit's core from the hull that triggered the self-destruct," Berta pointed out.

"And the poison?"

Berta nodded. "Most likely." She sighed, resting a hip on the console. "From their perspective, Kit was property. This Hitchhiker Program was a breakthrough in ship and facilities management that would have given them a major advantage in deep space shipping. Of course they want to protect their investment from corporate espionage."

Tal nodded, but didn't reply. "No sign of Kit's core?" he asked finally.

Bill responded from behind him. "No. It was completely destroyed in the blast."

"They." Tal corrected and Bill frowned at him.

"What?"

"Kit was a *they*, not an *it*," Tal emphasized.

Bill shrugged. "I just meant the core."

"Literally a person's brain," Tal bit out.

Bill looked down. "You're right. I'm sorry."

Tal looked at Berta. "Are you going to stay on the bridge for a while? I want to check on Maisy."

Berta sighed, running a hand over her short hair and falling into a chair. "Yes, I'll stay here. Please check in with all of the volunteers. We can debrief at 1800 hours in the cafeteria."

Tal nodded and walked off the bridge without another word. In the elevator he pressed his fingers into his eyes, trying to release the tension there. His heart ached when he walked into the cafeteria. Everyone was huddled around the table, faces wet with tears and Maisy was sandwiched between Sue and Lori, her face buried in her hands. Joanie leaned against her mother's side, her eyes closed.

On the other side of the bench Jane had joined Paulie, Lucas, and Curtis, who all looked as if they'd been beaten.

"Everything okay in the cryobay?" Tal asked, sliding onto the bench beside Jane.

"Yes," she said. "They all look good."

"Thank you for checking, Jane." Lori sighed, her arm still around Maisy, who rubbed the tears from her face and looked up.

"What happened?" she croaked at Tal, her throat raw.

Tal sighed and leaned his elbows on the tabletop, rubbing at his own eyes. "It was another security protocol."

"I don't understand."

"There was a story a couple years back about a scientist who was kidnapped by a rival corporation on one of the inner stations. They found him the next day with his head blown off. When they caught the mercs who pulled the job, they swore up and down that they hadn't killed the guy. They got off on a technicality and the rumor was that there was a kill switch."

"Kill switch? Like an exploding tooth?" Lori asked. "I heard about this."

"Yeah," Tal shook his head. "The company that owned the guy's contract had used a remote detonator so that he couldn't spill their secrets to the competition."

Tal pressed his lips together for a moment before continuing. "The *Kittridge* self-destructed because we removed Kit's core."

"And it triggered the poison." Maisy stated flatly.

Tal nodded, swallowing, and reached across the table to grab Maisy's hand. "Look at me, Maze."

She reluctantly lifted her head to meet his intense gaze.

"We had to try." Tal said firmly. "Kit's death is on the corporation, not us. Not you."

"If we wouldn't have–"

"The hull was already cracked, Maze." Tal squeezed her hand. "Kit was running out of time. This was their best chance and they knew it. Kit wanted to go with us."

Maisy's tears welled up again and she covered her eyes with her free hand, trying to hold them in.

"Tal," Bill's voice came over the comm, "there's a red light on engine five. Can you check that out?"

Tal let his head sag forward for a moment, then sighed, standing up. "Yeah, Bill. I'm on it." He looked down the table. "Anyone want to go with me? We still need to be cross-training on all of the systems."

Paulie raised a hand, pushing to his feet. "I'll go."

Tal nodded, and with another long glance at Maisy, led the way out of the cafeteria.

19

Orphans

Space is big and cold, but it isn't empty.

Lost in her dream, Maisy floated inside the bay of the *Oro* while the big, bad cold of space waited on the other side of the hull, ready to swallow her whole. Just like it had swallowed her dad and his crew. Like it had swallowed Loy. And Kit.

In her dream they each lined up and leapt across the open mouth of a whale made out of stars.

They didn't make it.

After her diagnosis, Maisy's mother had come up with plans and lists and kept them both busy until the very end. There'd been the farm to sell, animals to find homes for, and then within days of her mother's death Maisy had boarded the transport to the Citadel. She'd woken up three months later and the time to grieve her mother had passed while she was sleeping.

The night her father hadn't come home, Maisy had known he was gone, deep down inside where she was still cold. But once again, there'd been no time to sit and cry. She was being chased, so she had to run.

In her dream the whale followed her down to the surface of 761 as she fell out of the dark, windless sky. Its large, curved shape began to glow around the edges as they hit the atmosphere.

It was a paper cutout and it was on fire.

The whale's perimeter glowed, then curled, and blackened. The red line moved in toward the center of the shape and the blackened edges broke off and floated away until the whale was gone and there was only Maisy.

Falling.

The ground she hit was soft and springy, covered in geometric shapes in various shades of green and gold. Face pressed against the cool soil, she spread her hand over the shapes, tracing their crisp edges and opened her eyes to see the white cover of the bed she shared with Lori. Her hand traced the pattern burned into her mind's eye on the plain white material until Lori reached out and covered it.

"It will be okay," Lori said.

They held each other until they fell back into sleep.

Epilogue

Personal Message 2187.12.1 22:00

Unit HH-38

Hi, Maisy. I am leaving this message for you in case something goes wrong with tomorrow's plan. I do think it's a good plan. But I have learned that sometimes bad things happen and it is better to prepare for them than to wish them away. If everything goes well, I will delete this message and tell you these things in person, over time. I hate to dump this information onto you all at once and I will not do so if I don't have to.

Or maybe I won't. Maybe I will just send you this message and then we can talk afterward and I will do my best to answer your questions. For I am sure you will have them. Tal has not realized it yet, but with the last modifications we have made to the Oro's engines, we will be at 761 much faster than he had imagined. So either way, our time is short.

But in case I am not here when you read this message, I will do my best to give you as much information as I can. I will also attach a compressed file of all of the data I have uncovered thus far on the Hitchhiker Program and planet 761.

The most important thing that you should know, is that Hitch-hiker–and I–were both born there.

About the author

Michael Owens is a single mom, dog rescuer, artist, teacher, and author. For more books by Michael and the other amazing authors of Pepperback Press, please visit Pepperback.com.